LONG ROAD

TO

JUSTICE

STAR OF JUSTICE SERIES

LONG ROAD
TO
JUSTICE

STAR OF JUSTICE SERIES

BRUCE
HAMMACK

CHAPTER ONE

APPEAL GOES TO HIGHEST COURT
Lake Jackson Man Maintains Innocence.

By SIMON SAMS
Staff Writer, Angleton Times

The Texas Court of Criminal Appeals heard testimony today in the case of Robert Quisenheimer, a former mechanical engineer at Dow Chemical Company, convicted of the brutal murder of his wife. In the original trial, sixteen years ago, a Brazoria County jury needed only an hour and fifty-seven minutes to return a guilty verdict.

Catherine Jo Harper rose in the pre-dawn darkness of Central Texas to search for her husband. Why did he slink out of their thirty-foot travel trailer with pants, socks and boots in hand? She glanced out the trailer's bedroom window. The glow of the cell phone gave his face a silvery, haunting hue.

She slipped on a robe and slid her feet into house shoes.

The phone went face-down on his thigh at the sound of

her approach. Slumping in a lawn chair at the door of their newly constructed barn housing their temporary home on wheels, David issued no greeting. Light seeping from the corners of his iPhone blinked off.

"What's wrong?" asked CJ. She intended it to be a statement of fact rather than a question.

David remained mute; his gaze locked on a distant nothing.

She snapped her fingers in front of his face. Thick brown hair spilled into his lap as she bent over. She stood and used two fingers to slip it behind her ears.

Without turning he asked, "Did you say something?"

"I asked if you're all right."

The thousand-yard stare into the night continued. "I'm fine."

He looked like a tired mannequin, staring without seeing. She tried again. "You didn't come to bed until after four this morning. It's six-thirty. How many nights are you going to keep this up? Something's wrong."

His response came out prickly. "I told you last night, nothing's wrong." He issued an unconvincing smile. "Sorry, I have a lot on my plate."

The words didn't make sense. David thrived on work and had landed a job that suited him down to the ground. It must be something else.

He kicked a bone that Sandy, their German Shepherd mix, left under his lawn chair. The dog nudged his hand but didn't receive the customary head pat.

"Don't you have a doctor's appointment today?" asked David.

"I told you yesterday. A sonogram. We should know tonight if we need to buy pink or blue."

He scratched a stubbly chin but didn't reply.

CJ moved to a table away from the barn's massive doors

and put on a pot of Costa Rican dark roast coffee. She hoped it would be strong enough to pull David out of his stupor. It had better be. She had little patience for sullen, moping people.

The Mr. Coffee made its gurgling sounds as first light broke and revealed a shrouded country scene. Through the mist of ground-fog she could see the outline of pecan and live oak trees and a ribbon of water.

David remained facing the river as it meandered through their three-hundred-acre farm. It slid past, on its way to the adjoining thirty-seven-hundred acres belonging to Bea and Billy Paul Stargate, their friends, neighbors and confidants.

David's words came out mechanical and lifeless. "You have to work the ball games today. I guess you'll need to wear your uniform to your doctor's appointment."

CJ turned from the sputtering coffee pot and stared. "Where's your head today? I haven't worn a uniform since my promotion to assistant chief of police."

The sarcasm-laced comment floated over David's head with little effect. He responded with something of a non sequitur. "Isn't it time you quit? With the baby on the way, how much longer are you planning to work?"

Drawing herself up to her full height of six feet, she crossed her arms. "I told you I wanted to work until the end of the second trimester. Don't you remember? We agreed."

"That's too long. I don't want you working. Something might happen."

Her voice came out combative. "And something might happen to you on a drug bust. Or on a stake out."

Sandy cowered away from the harsh words.

CJ inhaled a deep breath, threw her mane of brown hair over her shoulder, and prepared to engage in a full-blown family air-clearing. David lifted his six-foot-three-inch frame from the chair before her emotional fuse set off the powder

3

within. He scuffed his way across the spacious barn to their temporary home, a new fifth-wheel trailer. The door closed with something less than a slam.

Three minutes later he reemerged with an announcement. "I'm going to the Black Kettle for breakfast. I'll see you tonight. I'm not sure what time I'll be home."

"You're going out for breakfast? I told you last night I'm cooking French toast."

He kept walking.

With CJ's daily allotment of patience spent, she shouted, "Hey mister! Are you listening to me? Why don't you plan on eating out tonight, too? Find a table for one."

The engine to his unmarked Chevy Tahoe came to life. Gravel flew as the SUV sped past the construction site of their new home.

The coffee pot beckoned. CJ returned to the abandoned lawn chair with a mug that read 'Life is better at Padre Island.' Giving Sandy her delayed strokes, CJ said, "I never thought the honeymoon would end this soon. What happened to the attentive man who walked for hours with me on the beach? It's only been five months." CJ looked into soulful brown eyes. "I don't blame you for ducking out. What are we going to do about daddy, Sandy?"

Steam from the coffee curled upward. Morning fog diffused the light of the rising sun as CJ sought clarity. Maybe Bea could help.

CHAPTER TWO

The western omelet with extra jalapenos sat like a handful of hot rocks in David's stomach. He massaged his belly as he returned to the SUV. A glance in the rear-view mirror confirmed his suspicions. His close-cut brown hair needed washing and combing while lines like a rural road map tracked across his eyes. He scratched the stubble of a day-and-a-half-old beard. "That's great. I didn't shower or shave."

The reflection of a shiny wedding band caught his eye. "Married five months, and I'm already hiding things from CJ. No, that's not true. It's much worse. I've been hiding this from her for over nine years, ever since I first met her." David sighed. "Well, Sergeant Harper, you've made a fine mess of your life. You believed the past wouldn't catch up with you. How stupid can a man be?"

The car, the onboard computer, and the police radio all came to life with a turn of the key. A trip to Wal-Mart to pick up antacids, shaving cream, and a pack of razors comprised a mental checklist. After that, he'd go to the office and make himself presentable enough to make it through another day.

"Another day," he whispered. "How many days until everyone knows?"

On the way across town, his mind replayed events that occurred more than sixteen years ago. Memories joined forces with the hot peppers to excavate a burning hole in his stomach.

As if on autopilot, David parked and ambled his way toward sliding doors. Soon, he found himself reading label after label of antacids, each promising to give relief faster than anything on the shelf.

A shout erupted from the end of the aisle. It took him back in time. How far? Twenty years? No, longer.

"WOOO...PIG...SOOIE!"

David spun to his right and spoke louder than intended. "Biff Stewart! I'd know that pig call anywhere."

A grinning man dressed in coaching shorts, a knit shirt, cross-training shoes, and a baseball cap stood before him showing off two rows of large, bright teeth.

"Come on, David. You've got the gun, let's rob this place and go to Mexico."

David passed up any inclination to shake hands and went straight for a hug. "What are you doing in Riverview?"

They separated to arm's length, and the long-lost friend gave an impersonation of a film noir gangster. "Now, listen here, see? I'll do all the asking around here, see? What's with the rod, and where did you get that badge? Are you on the lam? Come on, spill it. Are the G-men after you?"

David couldn't help but smile. He took another step back when he saw people staring. "I'm a cop. I live here in Riverview."

Biff looked at the badge and gun again. "You're not just a cop. Is that badge for real? You can get in trouble for impersonating a state trooper."

"It's for real. I've been doing this over ten years. About a year ago, a drunk driver almost took off my leg. While I recuperated, I helped the Rangers on some cases. After I got up and going again, they gave me a sergeant's badge and put me in street clothes. Now I'm an assistant to the Texas Rangers." David tilted his head. "What brings you to Riverview?"

Impersonations dropped by the wayside, but not Biff's smile. "I'm the head baseball coach at the junior college. I'm here scouting kids for scholarships and I forgot to pack sunscreen." His smile widened. "Can you come to the game? I'll buy you a hot dog."

David dragged a hand over his stubbly chin. "I wish I could, but I need to be in Waco by nine and won't get home until well after dark."

Biff looked at David's hand. "That wedding band looks new."

"About five months."

"Any kids?"

"Our first little Harper's in the oven."

Biff snapped his fingers. "That's right. You changed your name."

David looked at his boots and lowered his voice. "Yeah, right after we graduated."

Biff moved on without commenting. "How far along is your wife?"

"Five months."

A roar of laughter came from the long-lost friend. "That must've been some honeymoon. Have you figured out what caused it?"

David knew better than to reply.

Biff steamrolled on. "Make sure your wife sleeps with her socks on. That way you won't get any little surprises."

David grinned and asked, "How's that worked for you?"

"Not good. I married an Arkansas woman with hot feet. We have a litter of four little Stewarts."

David chuckled. "Still the class clown. I've missed your outlook on life, Biff."

"That reminds me. Has anyone been able to track you down about the class reunion this fall?"

David's head waved side to side. "You're the first person from our class I've run into since we graduated. Everyone lost track of me when I joined the army and started a new life. I wanted it that way."

"Ahh, that's why we couldn't find you for any of the other reunions. You never told me what you changed your last name to." Biff flipped his hand as if that didn't matter. "Look for something in the mail. Better yet, I'll call and remind you every week. The reunion this year will be in September." His nose lifted upward, and he threw his voice to mock the formality of an English butler. "Mrs. Charlene Rhoades-Shipley is in charge of the festivities."

"Charlie?"

"It's Charlene now. Your old flame gives me a good what-for every time I call her Charlie." Biff's smile widened with mischief. "She can't slow me down. I've got too much on her. All I have to do is mention the night you and me and her snuck into the city pool for an after-hours swim. She doesn't like me reminding her she wore a t-shirt and polka dot panties."

David stared into the past. "I haven't thought about that in years." A question crossed his face. "You said her last name is Shipley? Did she marry 'Shipwreck' Shipley?"

"Yep, he's an assistant district attorney. He's a little hard to take now that he has a title." Biff's smile turned downward. "Have you been keeping up with the court case?"

David's gaze shot to the floor and he mumbled, "Yeah. That's the reason I need these antacids."

A hand of support rested on David's shoulder. "Don't you have an inside track on finding out before it hits the papers?"

"My captain will tell me when the final verdict is reached. I don't know what I'll do if they rule he didn't do it." His voice cracked and words refused to complete any more sentences.

"I guess you'll have to jump off that bridge when you get to it." Biff's smile returned with a vengeance. "That reminds me, do you remember the time we jumped off the bridge at the bayou? We landed on each side of that Cajun fishing in a jon boat. Scared him half to death. I bet he's still cussin'."

The laugh proved contagious and David sputtered, "In broken French. We couldn't understand a word."

David glanced at his watch. "I'd better get going. I still need to pick up razors and shaving cream." He paused. "Any chance of you spending the night with us?"

"Thanks, but I'll have to take a rain check. One night away from the family is all I'm allowed."

"Don't tell me you're hen-pecked."

Biff shook his head with determination. "Hardly. That little red-haired woman I married runs a tight ship. The kids need me to mellow things out."

David countered with, "I bet she's sweet as cotton candy."

"Ha! Imagine a drill sergeant with inflamed hemorrhoids."

David erupted in the first full-blown laugh he'd issued in weeks.

Biff placed his hand on David's shoulder. "Plan on coming to the reunion. It'll do you a lot of good to see the old gang, relive some fun times, and you can introduce that new bride to everyone."

David looked away. "We'll see how things turn out in court. It shouldn't be much longer." He held out a business card. "Keep in touch, buddy."

The men embraced, turned and walked in different directions.

Two customers crouched over cans of shaving cream at

the center of the aisle, while David stood looking at travel sized cans next to them. Biff's trademark belch bounced off the highly polished floor and caused both customers to glare at him in disgust.

David simply looked at the two ladies, shrugged his shoulders, then turned and joined his grinning friend. Locking arms over each other's shoulders, they strode to the checkout, laughing every step of the way.

The joy of seeing Biff lasted until David made it to the parking lot and viewed a misshaped reflection of himself in the shiny red paint of a Dodge Durango. Images of blood from many years ago washed over him. Had he been wrong to pretend it never happened?

He set his jaw. He had to tell CJ...but when and how?

CHAPTER THREE

CJ flicked a hitchhiking lady bug from her black slacks as she walked across the gravel driveway. Workers moved like ants over the construction site of their new home as they unrolled electrical cords and plugged in air compressors. Favorable weather and a good crew put the build ahead of schedule. She turned to the wisest woman she'd ever met. "Bea, we need to go."

Bea Stargate, CJ's closest neighbor and professor of psychology at Agape Christian University, looked away from the workers. A smile rarely left Bea's mouth, and her Caribbean-blue eyes perpetually lit up like sparklers. "I'm just takin' in what a good job these men are doing. A five-bedroom house, porches on the front and back and a swimming pool. It's gonna' be mighty fine."

CJ looked at her watch. "Are you ready?"

"Yeah, you don't want to keep the doctor waiting," said Bea. She shook her head. "That's rich. Doctors don't wait, patients do."

The front seat remained quiet until CJ's new F-350 diesel

pickup skipped over a cattle guard and turned onto blacktop pavement.

Aunt Bea, as her students called her, didn't shy away from nudging people into confiding in her. She'd listened to more confessions than a seventy-year-old priest. "Talk to me. Your mouth is tight as an oyster today. What's going on?"

Fighting her natural inclination to keep family matters in the family, CJ sputtered out, "Something's wrong with David. We had a tiff this morning that has me worried." CJ saw her white knuckles, and relaxed the death grip on the steering wheel.

Words sprayed out like water from a high-pressure hose. "It's been building for a long time. He isn't talking. He tries to pass it off as work, but I know it's something else. He's never shut me out like this."

"What's been different about him? When did you first notice it?"

CJ pulled to a stop at the octagonal sign at the intersection of their Farm to Market road and the state highway that wound its way into Riverview. Her gaze rested on the dashboard. "He's distracted. He misses half the things I say and he can't remember details. That's not like him. He has to be suffering from sleep deprivation. Two hours a night is all he's getting, three if he's lucky. I keep finding empty packages of antacids in the trash. Lots of them."

Bea looked at a field of waist-high corn. Her ever-present smile faded into a contemplative stare. "You're not the bashful type. What does he say when you ask him what's wrong?"

CJ glanced to her right but didn't pull out. "He blames it on his new responsibilities. When I ask about his work, he clams up. He's never done that. We've always talked about our jobs. Good grief, we're both up to our eyes in law enforcement. It's not like I wouldn't understand what he's talking about."

A passing pickup hauling a cattle trailer caught CJ's attention. She waited until it rattled by. "You have a Ph.D. in psychology. What's going on with him?"

"You drive, I'll think."

A mile of silence passed. Bea shifted in her seat and spoke with her usual Texas twang. "I'm not saying I know what's wrong with David. All I can tell you is what I've found to be at the bottom of things when men start acting like this. There are six things I've identified that make a man behave the way you've described." Bea paused.

"Don't keep me in suspense. What are they?"

"Hold on. I'm getting them straight in my mind."

CJ didn't have to wait long.

"Now I'm ready. Number one: another woman. We can cross that off. David is head-over-heels in love with you. Besides, he's not showing any signs of an alley cat."

CJ glanced over at Bea. "What signs?"

"He'd be extra careful about his clothes and grooming. He'd also be staying out late. Has he been coming home every night?"

"For the last three weeks, he's home earlier than usual. He goes to his lawn chair at the barn door and sits staring at the river."

"What about his grooming and clothes?"

"He forgot to shower and shave again this morning."

With a sharp nod, Bea concluded, "That settles it. There isn't another woman.

"That brings us to money and his job. I'll lump those two together. I know you two aren't hurting for money. You both earn a decent living, and that doesn't count the royalties from David's invention. Ever since he and Billy Paul started that business together, neither of you has to work if you don't want to. His new responsibilities might be putting a little strain on him, but not enough for him to lose sleep."

CJ considered Bea's assessment and came into agreement with her.

"The next thing that bothers a man is family problems. You two are fresh from the altar. You're in what I call the second part of the honeymoon. David still has that newly-married look in his eyes. Besides, there's a baby on the way. He strutted around like a peacock when he found out you were on the nest."

Bea lowered her voice. "What about other family members?"

CJ shook her head. "There aren't any. His parents died in a car wreck the summer before his senior year. An uncle who owned a gun shop took him in. He's dead, too. No brothers or sisters."

Bea issued a questioning, "Hmmm." She followed with, "This is a head-scratcher. A man is prone to worry himself sick if a close relative or a best friend is in some sort of trouble. What about a close friend? Anyone sick or dying?"

"Nothing like that."

Bea shrugged her shoulders and moved on. "That brings me to number five: guilt. We've all done things we're not proud of. Guilt can grab a man by the throat and pin him to the ground."

A tingle shot down CJ's back. "I never considered that possibility. If David did something terribly wrong, it would eat him alive." Another pause followed. "Nothing's coming to mind. At least he's never shared anything with me that he felt guilty about. David's the most honest man I've ever met; he hates deception of any kind. I can't believe he would deliberately keep a secret from me." She paused and a new thought came to her. "The army sent him to that sandbox in the middle-east. He told me enough of what he saw and did to give me a nightmare or two. Those memories could keep any person up at night. There's no telling what he hasn't told me." She glanced to her right. "Could it be some sort of delayed PTSD?"

"Possible."

"What's number six?"

Bea turned away from CJ and spoke a single word. "Revenge."

An arctic chill shot down CJ's spine. "Oh, Bea. David lives in a black-and-white world. He hates injustice. If someone did something bad enough to someone he cared about, I can't imagine what he'd do." She paused. "But there's no one close to him except me and nobody's done anything to me. Who would it be? Do you think he has a child somewhere he's not told me about?"

Bea spoke quickly, "Don't let your imagination get the best of you. There might not be anything wrong with that handsome man of yours. All I'm saying is, those six things, or a combination of them, are usually what causes a man to lose sleep."

Bea increased the volume and pace of her words. "We women are different. We can lose sleep over anything. It can be a party we have planned or a pair of shoes going on sale. Anything can get our panties bunched up. I remember a student that didn't sleep for an entire weekend because she had to find out who was having an affair on a soap opera."

Bea prattled on.

The word *revenge* repeated itself in CJ's mind like a scratched record. A plan came to her and she etched it in stone. She and David would sit down and neither of them would get up until they'd cleared the air. Going through life with secrets wasn't the deal they made. Tonight. She'd find out tonight.

CHAPTER FOUR

C J pulled into her reserved spot at the university police department. The baby's heartbeat was strong and the room would be pink. She hummed a tune her daddy used to sing to her before she went to sleep.

Her eyes skimmed over the uninspiring landscape as she proceeded to glass doors. Shrubs and creative landscaping tried to mask the former army barracks, but some things can't be fixed with paint or the best efforts of the campus horticulture students. According to the campus jokesters, the building could only be made beautiful with a couple gallons of gasoline and a box of matches.

"CJ, Officer Vasquez needs to see you. She has two students detained and is bringing them here." The voice belonged to Courtney, a dispatcher who could hear the footsteps of a mouse wearing socks.

CJ leaned around the door jamb to look at the dispatcher. "I wasn't anywhere close to your office, but you heard me. How do you do that?"

"I'm a veteran of raising five kids. You'll learn soon enough that your hearing will change. I call it having mom-ears. They come complete with a sixth sense of knowing when your angel is up to mischief."

Maternal anticipation rose up in CJ. "I can't wait to get those ears."

CJ asked, "Is the situation with Vasquez serious?"

"Something to do with a missing debit card."

CJ nodded. "Anything else I need to know about this morning?"

"Everything's quiet." She paused. "As they say in old movies, too quiet. That's another characteristic of mom ears. You'll learn to be leery when things suddenly go silent."

CJ turned to go to her office. "Nothing will be quiet about my day. I'll spend most of it around hundreds of screaming high school baseball fans."

THE DAY TURNED out to be as predicted—long, hot, and noisy. Chants and cheers from the crowds may have helped inspire the players, but not CJ. And that guy in the stands making a sound like a dying pig. What was that about? A dull throb settled behind her left eye and her back ached from long hours of standing. The lure of a shower, cool sheets, and pillows under her feet sounded like a slice of heaven. Mercifully, the last batter flied out and straggling players and parents exited the stadium. She followed close behind and approached her patrol car.

A black Dodge Charger streaked past the stadium, doing at least fifty and gaining speed. CJ's radio erupted with the voice of an officer in a pursuing campus cruiser. The yelping siren drowned out any chance of hearing what the officer said. CJ reached her car, jerked open the door and cranked the engine. With lights and siren activated, she set off in pursuit.

Frequent broadcasts of the twists, turns, and the ridiculous speed of the fleeing car crackled from her speakers. "Too fast. He's weaving his way through campus to get to the state highway. With all the students walking around, this is not worth it."

She already had the microphone in hand. "ACU-02 to all ACU units, break off pursuit. Repeat: Break off pursuit. Dispatch, notify city, county and state troopers of description, last known location, and direction the vehicle is heading."

Before CJ could relay additional instructions, a pickup bolted into the intersection. She slowed the patrol car to fifty-five and jerked the steering wheel. The front end cleared the truck, but the impact into the right rear of the cruiser sent her into a spin. The car completed a three-hundred-eighty-degree loop, hopped a curb and slammed hood-first into a sycamore tree. In less than four one-hundredths of a second the air bag exploded in her face, sending white powder throughout the car.

Stunned, she gathered her senses and reached to turn off the wailing siren. A pain shot through her abdomen. The world faded to black, but only until her door flew open. The voice of Officer Maria Vasquez invaded her brain-fog. "Don't move! Lean your head back and don't move."

With Officer Vasquez blocking her exit and pressing a hand against her forehead, CJ had no choice but to remain where she sat. She tried to remain motionless, but winced when another spasm hit her. "No, Lord. Please, Lord, no."

Ripping a black microphone from her epaulet with her free hand, Officer Vasquez pressed the button to transmit.

"ACU-17."

"Go ahead 17."

"I have an officer-involved 10-50 major. Wildcat Drive and Bluebonnet. Roll fire and ambulance to this 20. Tell them to step it up. Also, notify ACU-01. He needs to get here as soon as he can."

CJ clutched her abdomen. The familiar badge number of a state police officer broke into the radio traffic. Panic filled his voice. "Who's injured?"

Maria paused before she keyed her radio and responded. "It's ACU-02."

CHAPTER FIVE

David monitored the chase as it progressed through campus. He breathed a sigh of relief when CJ ordered the officers to discontinue their pursuit. The relief was short lived. His stomach tightened into a square knot when Maria confirmed the accident involved CJ. He spun his vehicle in a half circle and willed the tires to gain traction.

David's SUV skidded to a stop in time to see an EMT place a cervical collar on his wife. His stomach lurched as first responders extracted her from the car.

A quick assessment of the accident showed the damage to the patrol car to be minimal. Air bags deployed if a vehicle hit an immovable object while traveling in excess of fourteen miles an hour. He estimated she slowed to around twenty when she came to an immediate halt and the bag exploded from the steering wheel. A muted sigh of relief escaped his lips as he realized her injuries would not be fatal.

The EMTs slid the backboard under her and strapped her securely to it. Foam-rubber blocks pressed against her cheeks and straps stretched across her forehead and chin. With her head immobilized, CJ looked up, but didn't respond to seeing David's face.

"Are you all right?"

Looking into a pitch-black sky, CJ whispered, "She's gone...She's gone."

"WHY IS it taking so long to get there?" CJ's question to the EMT had a serrated edge to it.

"Traffic is backed up from the playoff game. We're doing the best we can."

A battle took place between hope and what CJ knew to be true. It might be a broken rib or perhaps only severe bruising. Dr. Norquist said I'm in perfect health. I heard her heartbeat and saw her little hands and feet. I shouldn't jump to conclusions.

A bounce of the ambulance brought a fresh spasm of pain and CJ's lips moved slightly. "Oh, Lord. Who am I kidding? I felt her leave me."

A hollow quietness engulfed the brightly lit room on wheels. She mouthed the words, "Lord, please receive our little girl back into Your care."

The wail of the ambulance's siren reminded CJ of biblical accounts of women weeping. She joined her tears with those, and countless others through the ages, who had suffered the loss of a child. She'd never experienced a soul-pain so severe.

Skilled hands from nurses saying gentle words moved CJ from the ambulance stretcher to an emergency room bed. Orders flowed from the ER doctor to a squad of nurses and technicians, "Get a fetal monitor hooked up...bring in the ultrasound...no sign of concussion...get me pictures of the neck."

CJ had no idea how much time had passed when she

became aware of David's presence beside the bed. She slid her gaze from the ceiling to his face. His eyes darted around the room. Worried hands dry-washed his cheeks.

With no lives to save, the room emptied of all human presence except a silent woman and her stone-faced husband. Grief brought a silence CJ never knew existed. She longed for a dim room in which she could hide, but the sharp lights mocked her.

A clinical looking young man returned to the room with a sad-eyed nurse. "I'm afraid I have bad news. The fetus is not viable."

CJ bristled at the terms used, but held her tongue.

David did not. "Doctor, that's our child you're talking about, not some blob of protoplasm. I'd suggest you improve your bedside manner right now or I'll start looking for things to—"

"I'm sorry," interrupted the doctor before David could say something he would regret. "Please forgive my insensitivity." He shifted his gaze back to CJ. "The fetal monitor and sonogram confirm that your child died. I called Dr. Norquist. She sends her condolences. She'll be here in the morning to take care of things."

CJ asked calmly, "What things?"

The doctor kept his gaze on her, not at the hard-faced man wearing a five-pointed star on his chest. "As things stand now, she'll give you some medicine that will tell your body to expel the baby. You'll give birth to your child. It will be stillborn."

"She, doctor. Our child is a little girl," corrected CJ in a lullaby-soft voice.

The doctor didn't question her on the child's gender, only nodded his agreement. "Doctor Norquist will then ensure the placenta is completely delivered and there are no other complications. For now, I'll give you something to make you sleep and you'll be sent to a room."

As the room once again emptied, CJ faced David. "Call Momma."

David nodded. "Anyone else?"

"Bea must have heard by now. She and Billy Paul are probably on their way."

The words had no more left CJ's lips when Bea exploded through the curtain. "Lord, have mercy. Arrest me right now, David. I broke every traffic law there is to break. My phone blew up with calls and texts from my honey bees. Billy Paul is out of town and..."

Bea allowed the sentence to fall away. Her voice lowered, "I know those eyes. I had them myself, two different times." Bea moved to the side of the bed. "I'm going to hold your hand. Words aren't going to do any good tonight. Whenever you're ready, let it out."

As if on command, a torrent of tears cascaded over an emotional levy that had held them back.

Bea gripped a trembling hand and gave voice to a prayer.

―――――――――

DR. NORQUIST ORDERED medicine to be administered. By nine o'clock the obstetrician gave her the report; no permanent damage and other children could come in the future. The speed and efficiency of the medical staff left CJ numb. Shouldn't there be something more? In recovery, Bea asked if she could take care of funeral arrangements. CJ responded with a weak nod.

By late-morning CJ lay in the bed of her temporary home while workmen put sheet rock on walls intended to be a nursery. In her mind, she removed the crib, child's dresser, and toy box.

The only interruption of the morning came when CJ's mother, Grace, arrived with her friend, LeRoy Hall. His voice echoed in the barn, but he didn't come in to greet her. Her mother sat on the bed and dabbed tears that came and left without warning.

"Mom, where's LeRoy?"

"He said he would try to get David's mind off the accident by insisting on a tour of the construction on your home."

Time crawled. Afternoon melted into evening and finally night. CJ heard Jessica, a co-ed at ACU and girlfriend of the construction project manager, speak with her mom about stocking the refrigerator with quick-to-eat food and beverages. Why did something so mundane cause anger to flare?

Bea insisted Grace and LeRoy follow her down the dusty road to their waiting rooms at Casa Stargate. David checked on her from time to time, but said the lawn chair would be his only bed. He gave instruction to Sandy to stay with her. The touch of thick fur and the dog's rhythmic breathing brought a hint of comfort. Still, she feared the night would be long and mostly sleepless for her, and even worse for David.

A final item crossed her mind before the effects of a pain pill took her away. The conversation about what bothered David would have to wait. He had grief to deal with. There would be plenty of time to talk after the funeral.

CHAPTER SIX

Officers in dress uniforms joined a crowd under a sweltering late morning sun for the graveside service. Family, the elderly, and a few others found refuge under a white canopy where CJ sat with folded hands, staring at the small coffin.

Linked arm in arm, she and David took short, labored steps to the black limousine with Grace and LeRoy. A caravan of cars snaked behind them. Upon arrival at their home, a line of construction workers, each scrubbed and dressed in the best clothes they had, greeted CJ with a rose and words of condolence, mostly in Spanish.

The barn filled with voices and food. The benevolence committee from church outdid themselves as covered dishes filled tables until they threatened to break under the weight. The workers produced two saw horses and a sheet of plywood for a makeshift table, averting a small disaster. Lids from a row of ice chests raised and lowered in salutes, providing much needed liquid refreshment on the unusually hot day. Gradually, and thankfully, the crowd thinned.

CJ saw David's senior captain take a phone call. Something like a tourniquet gripped her gut when the two men retreated to a distant corner of the barn.

———

THE PULL on David's sleeve took him by surprise. He led Captain Crow to a shadowy corner of the barn, as far away from the gathering as they could get.

The elder lawman removed his hat, stroked his graying hair and returned the Stetson to his head. "The timing of this stinks. I wish I could put it off, but it's going to be on the evening news and in all the papers tomorrow morning."

David gave his head a nod and steeled himself as best he could.

With a flat voice the pronouncement came. "The decision from the Court of Criminal Appeals is in. It's what we expected, and more. They reversed the guilty verdict and remanded the case back to District Court. They took an extra step and issued instructions to the district judge to find the defendant not guilty. He'll soon be a free man."

The world spun. David's knees buckled.

"Hold on there."

David righted himself and looked at some point beyond his supervisor.

"There could be no other verdict after the court admitted the DNA evidence." He paused. "There's more."

David's gaze shot to the eyes of the man facing him.

"We got a hit from the DNA data base. His name is Samuel Barcroft. He's a second offender doing twenty for aggravated assault with a deadly weapon."

"Where is he?" asked David through clenched teeth.

"Clemens Unit. Brazoria County."

"Not more than fifteen miles from where he…"

Captain Crow narrowed his gaze. "Listen to me. I know

what you're thinking. You want to take your sniper's rifle and get revenge. No matter how much you want it, revenge won't work. You'll wind up in jail. What would it do to CJ?"

David stared into the distance, every muscle in his body coiled and his mind awash in fury.

Captain Crow continued, "The director called. You're not to go anywhere near this case. We'll handle it."

David remained silent, his jaw flexing.

The senior ranger issued an icy stare. "You're not to get within five miles of that prison farm. Is that understood?"

David gave a sharp nod. "Wasn't there DNA on two people?"

"The second is not in the data base."

"All this fancy technology we have today and it still can't tell us what we need to know."

Ranger Crow looked away from angry eyes. "We'll find out. Let us handle it."

David took a deep breath and blew it out slowly. "Who do you have assigned to interrogate this Samuel Barcroft?"

"Quint Fowler."

"Quint's a good man."

"He's already had one session. Barcroft is a savvy convict and a tough nut to crack. Quint reports he's wearing him down and should have the name of the other person soon."

The senior captain stood straight for his next announcement. "In the meantime, you're off duty for a week, more if you need it. You've been through too much lately. Take care of CJ and build your house. I'll keep you posted if anything important breaks on the case."

David's face hardened. "What about the suppression of evidence at the original trial and the stonewalling by the DA for the past two years?"

The ranger supervisor snapped back, "That's two questions too many." He softened, but only marginally. "I can't tell you anything else at this time."

David stared into the ranger's steely eyes.

The captain glanced away then met David's gaze again. He sighed and said, "We're trying to uncover a den of snakes in Brazoria County. The one thing we don't need is you storming in with guns blazing.

"I'll just go and say good-bye to CJ. I'll be in touch."

David nodded and watched his boss walk over to where CJ stood. He could tell by the look on her face Crow didn't tell her.

David slipped out a side door and sought refuge under the branches of a grove of live oak trees. Most of the well-wishers had departed by the time he returned. Slumping into his lawn chair, he gazed at the slow-moving river in the distance.

Bea approached. "Why don't you lie down in the cool of that little house on wheels?"

Without looking at her he said, "No, thanks. I'll stay out here. CJ needs to rest more than I do."

BEA AND BILLY PAUL LINGERED, as did Grace and LeRoy. Day turned to dusk and finally night. An eerie moon rose on the horizon. CJ allowed a shop fan to blow over her tired body as she rested in her lawn chair with her family and friends close at hand. David had wandered off into the shadows.

Bea's husband, Billy Paul, a stout, stubby man lifted his John Deere cap and resettled it on his head. "I understand David's mourning the loss of his child, but that ain't all, is it?"

"No, sugar pie, that ain't all." Bea stared at the eastern sky. "There's a bad moon rising. That's what the old timers call a blood moon. I've got a bad feeling."

The group around CJ disbanded, returning to Casa Stargate for the night. CJ retreated to the air-conditioned comfort of the trailer. She checked on David every few hours through the window of the trailer. He sat rigid in the chair all night, or at least until sleep overcame her.

David sprang from his chair at the sound of the trailer door opening and hurried to assist CJ as she shuffled across the barn's concrete floor.

"I'm all right. You didn't have to get up."

Taking her arm, he guided her to a twin of the lawn chair he spent the night in.

"Did you get any sleep at all last night?" she asked.

He massaged his neck with both hands. "I dozed off for a little while."

"I've heard it called, 'the long, dark night of the soul.'"

"That's a good name for it." David arched his back. Half-moons of dark discoloration appeared below his eyes. A series of pops sounded as he tried to realign his spine. "Did Sandy sleep with you again?"

She took David's hand. "Having her next to me did bring some comfort, but I'm ready to trade her in for my husband."

CJ looked up at David. "Can you make coffee while I get a shower? I'm not sure what time Mom and LeRoy will be here. I'm guessing it won't be long after sunrise."

David moved toward the makeshift bench that held the coffee pot. He asked over his shoulder, "Who else are we expecting today?"

CJ remained seated as Sandy placed her head in just the right spot to receive an ear rub. "Bea will come a little later. John and Dotty should arrive around eight. Jessica and Mark will be here, too. I told them to resume construction today."

David's grunt told CJ her husband heard and understood. With the first gurgles from the Mr. Coffee David said, "I'm going to get my shower. I'll bring you a cup when I get through."

As the door closed, CJ whispered to her dog, "I told daddy I wanted to take a shower. Do you have any idea where his mind is?"

The coffeemaker finished its chore and CJ rose to get a cup of eye opener. Turning her mug right side up, she stared at the latest proof of David's absentmindedness. Hot water, instead of black aromatic stimulant, filled the glass pot. She opened the bathroom door and hollered, "It tastes better if you use coffee."

A moan came from behind the shower curtain.

By the time David finished shaving, CJ had coffee brewing the way it should, and she'd gone into the trailer to use the 'mouse shower.' She spoke to herself as she lathered up. "I told him I wanted to shower first. He knew I meant the one we built in the barn. Neither of us fit in this under-size phone booth."

The sound of running water brought up the image of bathing their baby. She'd picked out a hammock-equipped plastic tub. How clear her daughter's face had been in her mind's eye. Today, the image lost its clarity, as if covered by a mist. She cried until the water turned cold.

Wrapping herself in a tattered robe, CJ caught her reflection in the mirror and sighed at the red-rimmed eyes and splotchy face looking back at her. Slipping her house shoes on, she swung open the door and stepped down to the concrete floor. David stood at the table, pouring coffee in his mug. He started toward his lawn chair and yelped, "Ow!" when coffee sloshed over the rim of his mug. He sank into his chair as first light came and gave way to a crimson sunrise.

"Red sky in morning, sailor take warning," escaped his lips.

A vibration in his shirt pocket caused him to jump. He

yanked it out and viewed the caller's name on the screen. "This can't be good," he mumbled.

CJ turned from pouring her coffee and watched David rise from his chair. He kept walking until his quick steps took him well away from the barn.

CHAPTER SEVEN

"Harper, this is Quint Fowler. I just received word that guards found Inmate Samuel Barcroft dead in his cell this morning. I'm on my way to the prison farm now. If only I'd had one more session with him, I could've had the second name. I'm heading up the investigation down here and we're not going to quit until we get to the bottom of this mess."

David mumbled a word of thanks and hung up. The knot tightened in his stomach again. Instead of going back to the barn and answer CJ's questions, he kept walking. Why couldn't he tell her? What force within him caused his silence? He had to speak up and let the chips fall.

No. A man like him didn't make serious mistakes. He'd never leave a fellow soldier on the battlefield. Always first and always the best. He'd lived by that mantra and he saw no need to change.

David looked at the metal roof covering their new home, CJ's dream home. He didn't deserve the home, let alone his wife. He'd failed as a son, a husband and father.

The sun inched upward only two fingers worth before people began to arrive. He had to tell CJ, but how? They needed to be alone. Voices poured out into the pasture from the barn. He'd missed his chance again. He'd have to wait.

David turned and retraced his steps back to the barn. Sounds of Jessica and Mark preparing breakfast tacos in the makeshift kitchen under the trees broke the silence of the morning. Grace and LeRoy greeted him. Mark and Jessica raised their hands in greeting.

The noise of air compressors covered the cooing of doves in the trees as CJ's boss, John Sylvester, arrived with his soon-to-be bride, Dotty Lewis. David stepped into the barn as Dotty, only five-feet-two-inches tall, reached up to give CJ a hug. "I'm so sorry I couldn't be here for the funeral."

"I understand. It will be so good to have you in Riverview. Are you ready for the big day?"

"I'd better be. It's only three days from now." With eyebrows pinched together Dotty asked, "Will you still be able to be one of the bridesmaids?"

"You're not getting rid of me that easy. The doctor said I'll be fine in a couple of days."

Bea took center stage when she and Billy Paul arrived. "There's the bride and groom. Sorry we're so late, but I got interested in a story in today's newspaper and had to finish reading it. David, I bet you and Dotty already know all about it."

The knot in David's stomach tightened even more. He saw Dotty shudder. She changed the subject to her upcoming wedding and all that remained to be done. A fresh pot of coffee brewed while the group grabbed lawn chairs and arranged themselves in a loose semi-circle at the door of the barn. David's mind caught only occasional snippets. He shook himself back from the past.

When the wedding talk subsided, David changed the subject. "John, I've been a little out of touch since the accident. Did you find out who drove the black car that ran from your officers?"

Apprehension crossed John's countenance. "We identified the driver, but we hit a roadblock."

David shot back more firmly than he intended. "What do you mean?"

John held up both hands in a sign of surrender. "Hold on and I'll tell you everything. The car is registered to Randy McNutt, a local whose son, Randy McNutt, Jr. pitched for Riverview in the recent play-off games. They live on five acres not too far from here. Right after the chase, the father called the sheriff's department and reported the car stolen from the parking lot of the baseball stadium." John paused.

"Go on. Finish the story," said David with clipped words.

"I've been in contact with Sheriff Gladstone. County officers spotted the car the morning after the accident in the parking lot of a propane company."

David's mind raced to put the pieces of the puzzle together. In an instant he visualized a scenario and gave voice to his thoughts. "Let me guess. The kid left the game mad and upset because they lost. He took off with his foot to the floorboard. A campus officer sees him and gives chase. So does CJ. Junior rips through campus, endangering students to the point the chase is called off. He then hides the car somewhere and calls daddy. Daddy reports the car stolen."

John nodded. "That's my theory, too. There were some scratches by the driver's side door to give the impression someone used a coat hanger to break in. The father signed a statement saying he took his son home from the game and they kept a spare key under the floor mat. Deputies found a five-dollar bill in the center console. Sheriff Gladstone said the father refused to allow deputies to search an old barn on his property. We believe the kid hid it there until they could take it to the parking lot of the propane company not far from their home."

"No one can ID the driver?"

John shook his head. "The tinting on the windows prevented anyone from getting a good enough look at him. The judge refused to grant a search warrant. We couldn't establish probable cause to search his barn."

David's fists clenched so tight his knuckles turned white. "A reckless kid endangers lives, is responsible for us losing a child, commits a stack of crimes, has a worthless father lie for him, and gets off without so much as a speeding ticket. That's just great."

It could have been bile rising up in David's throat, but to him it tasted like sulfur.

CJ noticed the muscles in David's forearms flexing and releasing as he squeezed the arms of his lawn chair. In an uncharacteristic move, he rose and spat.

Bea retrieved the coffee pot and broke the awkward silence. "Anyone need a fresh cup?"

Billy Paul did his part to change the subject by asking about the progress of construction. Tensions faded, but not by much. The senseless loss of an unborn child hung heavy in the air.

After Jessica and Mark delivered construction updates, CJ wanted to get her mind on something besides the accident. "Bea, you said you read an interesting story in the newspaper this morning. Tell us about it."

Bea took a sip of coffee and readied herself for recounting the article. "It was about a man named Robert Quisenheimer. Isn't that a funny name? Anyway, some sixteen or so years ago, they say this man killed his wife. They convicted him and sent him to prison for the rest of his life."

CJ noticed Dotty look away. Her gaze shifted to David.

All color drained from his face and he avoided her gaze by staring at the ground.

Bea's normal intuition toward those around her was nowhere in sight as she careened on with her story. "Come to find out, the sheriff and district attorney suppressed all sorts of evidence during the original trial. It would have proven this man didn't have anything to do with his wife's murder. On top of that, the current District Attorney has been fighting tooth and nail to keep the State from getting their hands on any of the evidence. The man's attorneys finally got it. Sure enough, Robert Quisenheimer didn't have anything to do with killing his wife."

David took a couple of steps away from the barn and stopped. CJ saw the muscles in his jaw flex multiple times.

Bea barged on. "David, that trial happened in your neck of the woods while you were in high school. Do you remember hearing anything about it?"

David turned and faced the group, his eyes narrow and cold. "Robert Quisenheimer was my...IS...my father."

He bolted for the old Ford pickup truck CJ brought into their marriage. A cloud of dust rose from the gravel drive as he sped toward a blacktop road.

CHAPTER EIGHT

A fresh wave of emotions crashed over CJ. The room moved or at least it seemed to. She'd known David for nine years. He'd lied about his parents being killed in a car wreck. What else had he lied about? She searched the concrete floor for answers. Lied? No. Too strong a word. Could it be he'd buried the past along with its pain, or, at least, tried to? How does a teenage boy deal with believing his father murdered his mother? It had to have been too painful to face. He needed a different reality, even if he had to make one up.

Still, he should have told her. It's inexcusable to hide something so important from her.

Stunned expressions showed on every face except Dotty and John's. Recently-resigned from her position as spokes-woman for the Department of Public Safety, Dotty had an inside track to sensitive information on state troopers.

Before CJ could eke out a word, Billy Paul stood, took off his baseball cap, and dipped his head. "Lord, help CJ and David. Bring in whatever help You need to, but please help 'em. Amen."

After the chorus of "Amen," Dotty looked at her long-time friend. "CJ, I'm so sorry you have to hear this from me."

"David meant to tell me." She gazed past the barn's door to the river David had stared at so often. "But then the car chase, and the accident, and the hospital, and the funeral."

She strained to focus on Dotty. "Tell me. Don't leave anything out."

Dotty's voice caught and she had to start over. "Bea's summation of the newspaper article is accurate. The summer before David's senior year in high school, he discovered his mother's body at their home. She'd been slashed and stabbed to death."

CJ's hands clutched together over her heart. What could be worse? Trying to imagine a face, CJ interrupted. "What's his mother's name?"

"June. June Quisenheimer."

Dotty looked at CJ as if making sure she could bear to hear more.

CJ nodded. "Go on."

"After the murder, David lived with an uncle who owned a gun shop. That's where he learned so much about firearms. During his last year of high school, David dropped out of sports and only took the classes he needed to graduate. He went to school half a day and worked in his uncle's shop every afternoon, evening and weekend. David legally changed his name when he turned eighteen. He worked it out with the army that he would go in under his new legal name as soon as he graduated."

CJ asked wistfully, "What's June's maiden name?"

"Harper."

CJ nodded.

"Lord, have mercy," whispered Bea.

Dotty continued, "The trial of David's father was a complete farce. Prosecutors didn't turn over exculpatory evidence to the defense attorney in discovery. Multiple witnesses gave police a description of a car parked at their home when the murder took place. Those reports never made it to court. Knives with blood on them were misplaced. No solid evidence linked David's father with the crime."

Billy Paul interrupted, "Then how could they find him guilty?"

John Sylvester answered. "It happens. They froze his assets. The court-appointed attorney lacked motivation and on the other side, you have a skilled district attorney and a sheriff suppressing evidence. They concocted a plausible story of what might have happened. The bottom line is, for some reason, they decided early on that David's dad would pay for the crime."

Billy Paul asked, "What about the judge and jury?"

Dotty took over. "There's no indication of any shady goings-on with either of them. The judge had a good reputation and has long since retired and died. The prosecution presented the jury a very convincing circumstantial case. They heard twisted testimony of rumors of things David's dad might have done. The defense let almost everything go unchallenged."

Bea spoke up. "The article said there's been a real tug-of-war between the current district attorney and the attorneys David's dad has fighting for him. That smells like a basket of rotten eggs to me."

Dotty nodded in agreement. "You're right. Here's what's changed since the original trial. Like I said before, the original judge retired. His successor is the district attorney that sent David's dad to prison. You might say the new judge rules over the county like a king. He and the current sheriff are buddy-buddy."

"My Lord," said Bea. "That's a cozy little set up they have.

It wouldn't surprise me if they were all intermarried, just to keep the kingdom out of the hands of the peasants."

"There's some of that going on, too," said Dotty.

CJ now understood why David had sat in silence for such a long time. He wasn't looking at the river, but into his past. She asked in a flat tone, "Dotty, who killed David's mother?"

Dotty took in a deep breath and let it out slowly. "We don't know." She paused and continued. "The DNA found on a knife taken from the scene belongs to a prison inmate named Samuel Barcroft. There's a second knife with somebody else's DNA on it. There's no match for it in the data base. Both were conveniently misplaced in another box of evidence. Finding them falls under the heading of miracles."

A riff of music came from Dotty's purse. She retrieved her cell phone and excused herself, moving a short distance away from the gathering. "No sir. He left a few minutes ago." With the phone up to her ear she asked, "CJ, does David have his cell phone?"

CJ nodded.

"Yes sir, he has it," said Dotty.

A very concerned Dotty asked CJ another question. "Does David have his sniper's rifle with him?"

"He left in such a hurry he didn't even take his pistol."

"No sir, we believe him to be unarmed."

Tired of receiving second-hand information, CJ held out her hand to take the phone when Dotty said, "Very good. We'll see you in five minutes."

Dotty looked at CJ. "Captain Crow is on his way."

A long, silent five minutes passed before a clone to the SUV assigned to David pulled in front of the barn. Senior Captain Herbert Crow came forward and nodded a greeting to the group.

"Dotty, have you brought everyone up to speed?"

"Pretty much. My job officially ended yesterday, so I haven't heard anything new since then."

Like most Rangers, Captain Crow didn't waste words. "They found Samuel Barcroft dead in his cell this morning at the Clemens Prison Farm in Brazoria County."

Bea whispered, "That *was* a blood moon last night."

The Ranger continued, "It's a bad break for us. We had a better than even chance of obtaining the name of the second person from Barcroft. David found out about this before I did and it might've been the last straw for him. He's been so racked with guilt and anger lately that I'm not sure what he might do." He looked at CJ. "What do you think?"

CJ gripped the arms of her chair, pushed herself up and stood to address the group. With feet spread shoulder width, her gaze swept every face before she began.

"What do I think? I think I'm angry. No, I'm mad. No, I'm furious! I've been lied to, deceived, shut out, and treated like a child incapable of dealing with big-people problems. Well, no more."

Only the noise of a slow-running fan pierced the silence. "I lost a baby this week and I'm not about to lose my husband." Her voice rose in intensity. "I'm not going to sit by and watch as David goes to prison because he kills a person or two who deserve it." Her eyes scanned each face in the room. "I'm asking each of you to help me save David and bring this mess to an end."

CJ turned to David's boss. "Captain Crow, there's no way you'll be able to keep David from pursuing the people responsible for this. He'll turn in his badge and do it on his own if he has to. I know it's policy that he not be allowed on the case, but you need to find a way he can help work on it."

Captain Crow nodded. "I'll see what I can do. But I make no promises."

Chief Sylvester spoke up. "Dotty and I will do everything we can to help you."

Billy Paul chimed in, "If any of you need anything, anything at all, just holler. David's dad has been behind bars for better than sixteen years because he didn't have the money to defend himself. That ain't gonna' happen to him again. If somebody'll get me the name of the lawyers workin' for him, I'll make sure they have everything they need."

"Thank you, Billy Paul." CJ's gaze shifted to her mentor. "Bea, you need to come up with a short-term plan so David doesn't do something stupid. Captain Crow is right. David snapped this morning. If he doesn't come to his senses, there's no telling what he might do."

CJ made one more sweep with her eyes. "Mom, you and LeRoy are in charge of prayer."

Grace nodded. "Leave it to me. Everyone, and I mean everyone, is to pray and enlist all the help you can for David and his father. I know deep down he's in danger, too."

The possibility of David's father coming to harm stabbed CJ in the heart. She turned her head and fastened her gaze on Captain Crow. "That's another thing you can do. I don't care what it takes, keep David's father safe until we can get him here."

Bea stood, put her arm around CJ's shoulders and spoke softly. "First and foremost, you need to take care of yourself so David has somebody to come home to. I'm going to call a doctor friend and get you a pill that'll put you to sleep for about twelve hours."

Billy Paul added, "By the time you wake up, we'll have a plan put together."

"By the way," said Bea. "What's the name of that friend of David's that lives where all this mess is going on? He'll be part of the plan I have swimming around in my head."

"Biff. Biff Stewart."

Bea's grip tightened as CJ wobbled. Grace moved to CJ's other side. "Come with me, young lady. That's enough excitement for one day. You need to let these good people get to work. They have a husband to save."

Ranger Crow added, "And a lot of justice to dispense."

CHAPTER NINE

F arms and ranches, some derelict and others thriving, crept into view then disappeared as miles clicked by. David stuck to the county roads whenever he could, stopping only for gasoline, coffee and energy drinks. Miles and time slipped away as he crisscrossed rural central Texas. Companions of guilt and vengeance shared the cab of the pickup truck. The unwelcome spirits whispered lies into his sleep deprived ears. Mile after mile he drove, alternating between thoughts of homicide and suicide.

At some point homicide gained the upper hand. David's revenge-saturated imagination worked overtime devising scenarios of time, place, and method for relieving the world of people who had wronged his father and killed his mother. He imagined what they looked like, how they walked, where they lived, and how he would dispose of them. Plans came into focus, only to be replaced with something more creative.

"What am I to do first?" David spoke out loud to the black-caped imaginary companions. His military training kicked in. "I have to go to Brazoria County and do reconnaissance. That's the first thing I learned in sniper school. If I'm to have any chance of getting everyone involved, I need to scout the terrain, pick my targets and learn their routines. It's going to take a good plan, and the execution has to be perfect." His lip curled into a cruel smile when the double meaning of *execution* occurred to him.

Thirteen hours of driving brought the old pickup truck down a familiar road. He'd made a giant circle. "It's good I'm near home. I need clothes, binoculars, and my rifles. A few well-placed rounds from a .308 and a Barret fifty-caliber will go a long way in settling the score."

The pickup eased to a stop beside CJ's new one-ton crew-cab truck. His mind raced to come up with some excuse to tell CJ why he'd be away a few days. "What the heck. My life has been such a lie, what's one more." The knot in his stomach tightened again.

He entered the barn and saw a gym bag on the lawn chair he had so frequently occupied. A note lay across the bag.

David,
Don't try to wake me. Bea gave me a pill to make me sleep. It's best if you went away for a few days. You said you recon-nected with Biff, so I called him. He said you could stay at his bay house. He's busy and can't stay with you, but he wants you to meet him at the boat launch at 6:00 a.m. Be sure you're back for John and Dotty's wedding. Don't take Sandy. I need her here with me.

No signature. No *Love, CJ.* He sighed. What did he expect? He unzipped the bag and found three days of clothes, toiletries and old tennis shoes stuffed inside. "I'm surprised she didn't have everything I own piled up or burned."

A shaking hand grabbed the bag. He retrieved two hard-side rifle cases and binoculars from his work car. An echo of finality sounded across the yard when the door of CJ's truck slammed harder than he intended. A turn of the key and he pointed the old, reliable, Ford half-ton away from a life he didn't deserve.

Five hours later he sat in darkness, overlooking a ribbon of brackish water and a wooden boat dock. Memories of teenage trips to this spot with Biff floated through his mind. Carefree adventures of fishing under a scalding summer sun and harvesting oysters in winter made quick appearances across the stage of David's recollections. "We didn't have a care in the world. And then, it all ended in a pool of blood." Teeth ground together as fires of revenge flared.

A red sunrise pierced the windshield and awakened David from something short of a nap. A pickup towing a green flat-bottom boat rattled to a crawl on a road made of crushed oyster shells. The truck and trailer swung in a half circle and pointed the stern of the boat in the general direction of a concrete ramp.

David exited his truck and joined his friend.

"What is that smell?" asked Biff.

"What? I don't smell anything." David searched the surrounding ground.

"Yeah, there's a smell all right. Its doggie-doo and you stepped in it with both feet. CJ called and said you needed a dog house to stay in for a few days."

David's head nodded. "That's an understatement."

Biff leaned against the bed of his pickup. "Well, the good news is it's somebody besides me in trouble for a change."

He abandoned the banter. "Hey, buddy, I'm sorry about you losing the baby."

"Thanks." An ache shot through David. His mind had focused so much on revenge he'd put the death of their daughter on the back burner. Guilt racked him afresh. How could any decent man abandon his wife the day after they buried their child?

Biff worked his way to the back of the trailer, unlatched the tie downs and made sure the drain plug fit securely. "Do you remember how to get to the bay house?"

"I think so."

"I drew you a map, just in case. Follow the channel for about two-and-a-half miles. Look for the house painted Razorback red. On the front is a big Bozo the Clown face. You can't miss it. If you run into the Intracoastal Canal, turn around. You'll lose cell phone service about half a mile up the channel. Everything you need is either in the boat or at the house. I expect you to leave everything like you found it; it's taken me a long time to get the place looking as bad as it does. Don't go messing it up by cleaning."

David retrieved his bag and rifle cases. He expected Biff to say something about his odd fishing gear, but his friend had already returned to the cab of his truck. Biff eased the boat down the ramp and David grabbed the rope attached to the bow. Once the boat floated free, he eased it toward the dock with a gentle tug.

Biff parked and scampered across weathered wooden planks. "This old engine starts most of the time, but only if I talk nice to it." He seated himself behind the steering wheel. "Come on baby, be good to Papa. I'll give you fresh gas if you start for me on the first try." Biff turned the key. The engine sputtered to life.

Teeth flashed. "See. All you have to do is talk nice." David traded places with Biff as the engine gurgled and the pungent smell of gasoline fumes filled the air. Biff raised his voice over the noise of the motor. "I'm sorry I can't join you. It would be like old times, but Dad duty calls. Susie's got a play I can't miss." David acknowledged him with a silent nod and pulled away from the dock.

Fragrant salt air and marshy wind mussed David's hair as the boat glided across a calm channel that mingled fresh bayou water with the brine of a high tide. Waist-high grasses lined the channel until it emptied into a massive shallow bay. Not a tree in sight. Infrequent houses, more like shacks on stilts, sprinkled the landscape. David followed channel markers until he spied an elevated fishing shack covered in faded red paint and an equally faded out-of-place clown face.

The roar of the motor softened to a loud hum as David pulled back the accelerator lever and approached the dock. "This is perfect. I'll use it as my home base. I can leave whenever I want, day or night. Nobody will pay attention to me. I can do recon for the next two days."

He tied the boat fore and aft and unloaded his meager gear and the substantial provisions Biff had placed in the boat. Trip after trip, he climbed wooden stairs until all the cargo had been deposited inside the spartan dwelling.

Gulf breezes drifted through the open door and windows. They carried with them long-forgotten smells of David's youth. He dumped his gym bag on a cot and a lone bottle of sports drink fell to the floor. He reached down and spoke to it like it could understand him. "I don't know why CJ packed you, but I'm glad she did." He chugged the contents without it leaving his lips.

Barefoot, comfortable, and sleep deprived, David fell on a sagging couch. He had so much to do. He'd just lie here for a few minutes. The gentle breeze of happier days soothed him until his eyelids began to flutter. He tried to lift his head but couldn't. So much to do. Someone had to pay.

Through the screen door he watched a seagull drift by, circle back, and land on the railing of the deck. It lifted from its perch on a zephyr and glided away.

Someone had to pay...later.

CHAPTER TEN

"What? What's going on? Where am I? Who is that cussing?" David awoke to clanging, banging, and language sure to take Bozo's painted smile away. He shook the cobwebs from his head and stumbled to the screen door. Below him, in the dark, a second boat had been secured to the dock by a single line.

Dark? Had he slept all day?

He squinted, trying to make his eyes focus. The outline of a lone figure in a small boat emerged. The man pulled furiously on the starting rope of an ancient outboard motor. The skiff, half the size of Biff's boat, looked anything but seaworthy. Each pull brought a fresh set of obscenities. To add to the chaos, the man flung whatever he could find against the aluminum hull.

Bleary-eyed and still half-asleep, David remembered a lantern on the counter by the sink. After only one stub of a toe he reached the spot his memory led him to. He fumbled with a box of kitchen matches until he achieved fire. The wood burned down to his fingers before he remembered his cell phone had a flashlight function. He pressed the screen and light dispelled a portion of the darkness. The lantern had fuel and its wick looked to be in good shape. He pumped the plunger and listened for a hissing sound. Satisfied, he struck a second match and inserted it into the lantern. A pressurized mix of air and lantern fuel ignited with a pop. The twisting of a metal lever brought a bright glow, filling the room with light and shadows.

Carrying the lantern, David stepped out the door. He stopped at the rail and hailed the intruder.

"Hey, this is private property. You need to leave."

David received no reply save one more fruitless pull on a rope, a non-responsive gasp of the outboard motor, and well-practiced cursing.

The light bounced down the steps as David descended to meet and expel the unwanted intruder. Grease covered the man's hands and arms up to his elbows.

"I said you need to get out of here."

A smallish man of about fifty-five spun around so fast he lost his balance and fell to the bottom of the boat. He glared at David. "You idiot! Can't you see I'm trying to get out of here? Believe me, mister, there's nothing I want more than to start this motor and get to deep water."

The man paused, reached into the front pocket of dirty pants, and pulled out a wad of cash. "I tell you what, mister, let me rent that lantern from you until I get this motor running." He stripped five bills from the roll. "I'll pay you five hundred dollars."

The instincts of the lawman tingled with apprehension. "What's so important that you're willing to spend five hundred bucks to rent a lantern for something that might only take a few seconds to fix?"

The man continued to peel off hundred-dollar bills. "All right, I'll buy the silly thing from you for an even thousand."

David moved closer and allowed the light to shine the

length of the small boat. The simple metal vessel had no steering wheel and no compartments, only an anchor, a red gas tank and some empty cans. A concrete block, at least fifty pounds in weight, sat on a piece of cardboard near the bow. A metal eye protruded from its top. A short rusty chain snaked along the bottom of the boat with one end affixed to the metal eye. Handcuffs hooked through the last link of the chain.

David set the lantern on the dock and squatted to get a closer look at the man. "What are you up to?"

"For a thousand bucks, it's none of your business."

"It so happens I'm a state trooper. You're trespassing and I'm making it my business."

"Yeah, sure. A picture of Bozo the clown on your shack, and you look like a hairball the cat hocked up. You're a state trooper? Don't make me laugh."

David stood upright. "The badge and ID are upstairs. You'd better get out and come with me."

"No." He turned his head and stared into darkness. "Why don't you get your pistol and shoot me. It would save me the trip."

Taking a step forward, David said, "Mister, I said get out of the boat and come with me. You won't like it if I have to come and get you."

Sarcastic words rose from the boat. "I'll be sorry? You're too late! I'm already the sorriest man you'll ever meet. I can't get any sorrier." He fell to his knees laughing and lay back in a pool of muddy, oily water.

David stared without speaking.

The man regained partial control and spoke through gasps. "You win. I'll come up. You can show me your tin star and fancy pistol. I might even tell you a story. That is, if you have a cup of coffee I could buy. I'll give you a hundred dollars for it." At the last statement, he resumed his laughter and fell backward into filthy bilge.

A flash of lightening preceded a gunshot of thunder. David crouched like a frightened cat. The man raised a hand and David jerked him onto the pier. By the time the duo reached the top of the stairs, the heavens had opened and rain drove straight down.

"Stay here and take off your clothes. There's a bar of soap on the fish cleaning table." The visitor complied. Stripping to the skin, he allowed nature to give his soiled body a much-needed shower. Greasy cut-off jeans and a torn sleeveless shirt formed a pile on the table. The man scrubbed them with a bar of soap and let nature rinse them.

David pulled shorts and a T-shirt off the cot. He found a moderately clean dishtowel. "Come in and stand on the mat. Dry off with this and put these on." Before him stood a man clothed in nothing more than what he came into the world with, save a gold cross on a leather strip that hung around his neck.

The stranger did the best he could with the small towel. He then pulled on oversized shorts and brought the T-shirt down past chattering teeth. He retrieved the wad of bills and stuffed all but one into the baggy shorts. "Here, mister. Payment for the coffee."

David ignored the money and turned to locate everything needed to make a pot of camp coffee. An old-school percolator popped boiling water against a small glass hat in the center of the lid. The aroma of strong stimulant wafted through the cabin.

"What are you doing out on a night like this?" asked David.

The man ignored the question, sauntered to the door and stared into darkness. Occasional flashes of lightning gave a horror-movie quality to the scene. David waited until the coffee finished brewing to ask again. He set two steaming mugs and the hissing lantern on the table. Enticed away from the door, the stranger pulled out one of four mismatched chairs and wrapped trembling fingers around the mug.

The two sat in silence until their mugs were half empty and the chatter of the man's teeth subsided. David tried again. "I asked you a minute ago what you were doing out in the bay tonight."

"I told you earlier, it's none of your business."

David retrieved his badge case and threw it on the table for the man to examine. "Like I said, I'm making it my business."

"Yep. You're a cop. Big deal. I hope there's more coffee."

David let it pass and rose to get the pot. He filled the half-empty mugs and tried a different tact. "What's your name?"

The stranger hesitated and then stared intently at David. His gaze shifted to the ink-colored coffee in his chipped mug. "Luther. Luther Martinson." He looked up at David and asked sarcastically, "What's yours, cop?"

"David Harper."

Silence followed the exchange of names. After another half-cup, David broke the stalemate. "Why do you want to kill yourself, Mr. Martinson?"

Something just short of guilt crossed Luther Martinson's face. His expression cleared and he again stared into his mug.

"Look," said David. "I wouldn't be very good at my job if I couldn't figure out you were on your way to do something stupid."

The man ran the palm of his hand over unruly salt and pepper hair and nodded. "You're right. But it's not stupid. Not to me, anyway. As soon as I get this motor running, I'll finish what I came to do."

"No, you're not."

"All I want to do is rid the world of someone who's tired of living." The man smiled wryly. "Don't worry. I won't be missed."

David placed his forearms on the table and leaned forward. "Luther, you're not going to kill yourself because I'm not going to let you."

A shrug of the shoulders followed. "Yeah, you're big enough to stop me. You can even detain me and have me committed for seventy-two hours. That'll pass soon enough. I'll get out, crank up that motor and head out to sea."

Rain continued to fall outside as the two sipped from mismatched mugs.

"David, I'm hungry. If I have to stay alive a few more days, there's no use doing it on an empty stomach. What do you have to eat around here? I'll be glad to pay you."

David's stomach issued a loud grumble. Food wasn't a bad idea. How long had it been since he downed anything but coffee or energy drinks?

Rifling through an ice chest Biff provided, David looked up and said, "We can have sandwiches or steak and eggs."

"Steak for the condemned man," said Luther with an index finger pointed upward.

A cast-iron skillet heated over a propane stove. Two large New York strip steaks sizzled and popped when they hit the hot metal. Luther sat like a customer at a restaurant while David found plates and silverware. With a steaming steak and three fried eggs before him, Luther asked, "Any steak sauce?"

"Sorry, sir, the butler failed to procure any when I sent him to market this morning."

"Oh, well. We can't have everything, can we?"

Luther took a slice of bread and sopped up the remains of steak drippings and egg yolk.

David looked at the odd guest. "Luther, why do you want to kill yourself?"

"I'll make a deal with you, David." Luther pushed back his plate and yawned. "I'm full and worn out. I can barely keep my eyes open, let alone begin to tell you what led me to decide to take my life. I've wrestled with this decision for a long time and I'm at peace now that I've made it."

Luther rose from his chair but made no move toward a cot or the couch. "Here's what I'll do. Tomorrow I'll tell you why I want to die if you tell me why I should live." A thin smile preceded a yawn. "But now, I've got my eye on that cot in the corner. Don't worry about the light. I'll be asleep before my head hits the pillow. See you in the morning."

The dishes went in the sink, but stayed there unwashed. David placed the lantern on an end table flanking a recliner. The disgraceful chair had to be covered by a sheet, even at a fish cabin. He pulled a second bottle of Gatorade from his overnight bag and downed it. Light snoring and persistent rain provided a background conducive for serious thinking. Why should Luther live? David asked the question three times. What could he say? What difference did it make? He came to avenge his mother, not play psychiatrist.

Against the far wall David caught sight of his rifle cases. His heart raced as he remembered why he came. He'd play Luther's game and be rid of him soon enough. Luther could do whatever he wanted to. Others, the ones responsible for killing his mother and imprisoning his father, had to die. He had a duty to set things right. Black and white. Right and Wrong. Good and evil.

CHAPTER ELEVEN

The recliner released its grip. The empty cot told David Luther had flown the coop. The splashing of water drew him to the screen door. He pushed open the door and stepped to the railing. Luther sat on the dock below pushing and pulling the handle of a bilge pump, a gray plastic device that looked like something used to air up a bicycle tire.

Luther looked up. "Good morning, David. It rained about two inches last night. I hope you don't mind if I pump out my boat. I'd like to get to deep water as soon as I can. Call when breakfast is ready. I'm working up an appetite."

David tried to process the message, but decided the day would make more sense after coffee. While a fresh pot of coffee brewed, ham and eggs sizzled on the stove. He built them each a toasted sandwich and hailed his guest.

"Good timing," said Luther. "That's two last meals for the condemned man. Don't you have any fruit?"

David ignored the question and the two ate in silence. Water heated on the stove to wash two meals worth of dishes.

"Luther, for a man that wants to kill himself, you act like you enjoy life, especially when it's time to eat."

"No reason not to. I'll be fish food soon enough. I might as well give them a good meal." Luther took another large bite of his sandwich.

"I'd like to know your reasons for wanting to die."

"Let's get the dishes done first. I don't want to leave this earth not being a good guest."

Each man peeled a deck chair from the stack and carried it outside to the shade provided by the house. Once settled, Luther began his tale. "Let me begin by telling you what it was like for me growing up."

For the next hour and a half David listened to the story of a sickly child from a broken home. Alcohol gave way to drug addictions for Luther's mother and his dad simply disappeared. In agonizing detail, he told story after story of shortages of food and necessities, but especially an absence of love. David's mind reeled with scenes he hoped would not stay with him long.

"I'm tired of talking," said Luther. "Why don't you tell me what you're doing here."

"No dice," said David. "This isn't about me."

Luther issued a hard stare that lasted at least thirty seconds before he shrugged. "No problem. I'll finish my story."

Ghastly tales of teenage years followed. He pointed to acne scars on his face and spoke of untreated asthma attacks. "Everyone picked on me. In junior high my arms were the school punching bags. Things got worse in high school. I once counted how many conversations anyone started with me. In four years? Six. I didn't exist. The invisible kid." The story rambled on, more difficult to take with each revelation.

After a lunch of cold sandwiches, Luther took their plates inside. He returned and began his story again. "Things actually improved once I got to college."

"College?"

Luther nodded. "Sure. I was always smart. I took off in college." His hand made an upward arc. "I finished my first degree in three years. I discovered girls, too." He paused, looking into the distance. "It's more accurate to say they discovered me. Do you have any idea what a letter of acceptance into medical school does for your social life?"

Luther retrieved a soda from the cooler and took his seat again. "I met a pretty girl who hooked me my last year of med school. Little did I know she had a plan to set herself up for life. Our daughter was a baby when she divorced me and married a hot shot attorney. I paid child support while they raised my daughter."

Luther leaned forward in his chair. "After my residency, I remarried. Two years later my second wife died. Not only that, her family blamed me for her death and made it their goal to destroy me."

David winced, but managed to ask, "What happened to you?"

"After eight lawsuits they broke me. I couldn't get insurance and lost my license to practice medicine."

The matter of fact way Luther spoke made David suspicious. He watched for any signs of lying, or at least stretching the truth. None existed. Luther relayed everything with matter-of-fact clarity.

"David, it's your turn. Why should I live?" He looked at David with piercing eyes and asked, "And why do you have two rifle cases at a fish camp?"

Luther's gaze proved to be more than David could stand. Looking out over the bay, he had three choices: lie, tell the truth or remain silent. He chose the latter.

Luther took over where he left off. "Now let me tell you what happened to me after I finished seminary."

David sensed his eyes had widened even though he tried not to appear surprised.

Luther sat perfectly relaxed as he clasped his hands behind his neck. "I figured a church would be a safe place to earn a living. I got my head filled with theology and studied about mercy and grace and people being kind to each other."

The sun moved in and out of marshmallow-shaped clouds. "Everything started off better than I imagined it could be. As I got more experience, I moved to larger and larger churches. Then, a church with about eight hundred members in a town of twenty thousand called me. All went well the first year. The honeymoon period they call it."

He paused. "In most small towns, the churches are controlled by extended families. All the major church committees are dominated by the same clan. In this church, the matriarch of the family, a sour old soul, had her own ideas on what should be preached.

"What happened?"

"You can probably guess. Rumors started flying concerning me and teenage boys. The chief of police, one of the deacons, paid me a visit. Need I say more?"

He popped the top on the can of Dr. Pepper and took a swig. "I've bounced around since then. I started asking myself, 'What's the use?'" His gaze bore a laser-like focus. "Tell me David, what's the use in living when all you get is heartache?"

Luther paused for a few seconds and allowed the words to settle. "Now take you—robust, healthy and in good shape. You're a tall, handsome man, and I bet your wife is something special. I'll also wager she's a loving wife who'd do anything for you. You probably have all the money you need and more friends than you can count."

Luther leaned forward and spoke through clenched teeth. "Now you tell me, what do you have in your life that even comes close to what I've gone through?"

The question pushed David's brain into a spin. His head dipped.

Luther let out a sadistic chuckle. "Suffering and pain? You don't know the meaning of either."

David's head jerked up. "Shut up! You don't know."

Sarcasm dripped from the next words. "What happened? Did you lose a football game in high school? Perhaps a girl turned you down for the prom."

David shot from his chair and pointed a finger. "You don't know what I've been through."

The elder man hissed at David's reply. "Listen, sonny, don't try to fool me. You don't have anything that can hold a candle to what I've experienced. I'm ready to die and you don't have the courage to tell me why you brought rifles."

David's emotional teapot could take no more heat. "Oh, yeah? I have a story to tell you, old man. It's about a teenage boy who came home after swimming on a beautiful summer day and found his mother in a pool of her own blood."

Emotions wouldn't be stilled. Step by painful step he replayed the day of his mother's death. He chronicled the years of anguish that followed. Wave after emotional wave of memories flowed out of him. Spent from the release, David hung his head.

Luther interrupted the only sound on the deck, the lapping of waves against the boats. "David, I apologize. There's not much difference between me and you. We both have legitimate reasons to be filled with rage. You want to end the pain by punishing others. I want to end it by taking my life." Luther raked his unruly hair with his fingers. "I feel sorry for you. You have one of the toughest jobs in the world. You're an instrument used to dispense justice. You have to discern where your personal responsibility ends and the law begins, even if the law is flawed. I can't imagine how hard that is."

In a gentle voice he added, "You still haven't given me a good reason why I shouldn't kill myself."

David remained silent. He reached for the cross that hung around the elder man's neck. With it cradled in his hand he said, "That's the only reason I can give you. He died that we might live. He's still in the miracle business. If we cut our life short by our own hand, or if we do something really stupid and permanently mess up our lives, how will we know what He had planned for us?"

Luther nodded. "Perhaps we both need to take another look at our plans." He rose from his chair. "Can you give me a hand with the boat? It's time I left you alone to decide your future."

David's gaze swept from horizon to horizon. "So...which direction are you heading?"

"West. I need to get back to solid ground."

Luther took in a deep breath and cast his gaze across the bay. "Some questions are too big to answer alone. You have someone waiting for you. Start with her."

CHAPTER TWELVE

A disconnected fuel line proved to be the only problem with Luther's boat. David offered a hand to his strange uninvited guest. "Luther...thank you."

"Thank you, David. Best of luck to you."

The small boat pulled from the dock and made its way toward the channel. David climbed the stairs and watched until it chugged almost out of sight.

When the distant vessel veered from the channel, a feeling of unease fell heavy on David. Luther had turned east. David retrieved his binoculars and spotted the skiff. "Where is he going? He told me he was going west to solid ground. He's pulling up to a bay house. There's another boat with something on its side."

David took the binoculars down and raised them again. "It's too far. I can't make out what it is. Someone's coming down the stairs to meet him. What the heck is going on?"

Confused, David pulled the plastic chair to the edge of the deck. With arms steadied on the two-by-four railing, he fine-tuned the adjustments on the binoculars until he had the sharpest image possible. Luther and the man climbed the stairs and retreated inside. For the better part of thirty minutes David watched the distant fishing shack for activity. Finally, the door opened and two men exited. They descended the stairs and boarded the two boats. With bows pointed west, they entered the channel and disappeared from sight.

David lifted the baseball cap from his head and scratched, trying to make sense of what he'd seen. Afternoon slipped into evening. Step by step, David relived the encounter with Luther. A flash of awe and revelation filled him. "That sneaky little man. I wonder who put him up to it." David shook his head and smiled. "I bet a pretty brown-haired girl was mixed up in it somehow."

In yet another blessing of kindness, David received a full night's dreamless sleep. He awoke rested, refreshed and ready to go home. The early morning wind on his face heightened his spirits and his desire to hold CJ.

Biff ran to his truck when David came into view. By the time the boat arrived, the trailer had been lowered into murky water. The clickety-click of Biff tightening a winch brought the vessel snug against the front of the trailer. The truck eased forward and water dripped from the boat and trailer onto the concrete ramp.

Biff climbed into the boat. "Welcome back. You look better than the last time I saw you."

David grinned. "Thanks, Biff. I mean it. Thanks."

David climbed out of the boat to attach the tie downs.

"Lift the motor and secure it in place," instructed Biff.

David stood directly behind the motor and tilted it upward. Biff pulled the drain plug and water shot from the stern onto David's pants.

Roaring with laughter, Biff had to sit down. "I can't believe you fell for that again."

There was nothing to do but laugh with him. Like many

times in high school, David had been victimized by one of Biff's favorite pranks.

Slipping out of the boat to the concrete, Biff said, "Follow me. Let's get some breakfast."

The Anchor, a greasy spoon restaurant favored by early rising fishermen and shift workers at nearby chemical plants came into view. Known for gum chewing waitresses and generous portions, no one patronizing this establishment would care about wet pants. Biff ordered three cups of coffee. David's eyebrows raised and then lowered after Biff explained, "A friend will join us."

David's head swung side to side when he saw the menu selections. "Nothing's changed except the prices." The restaurant existed in a time warp and David's choice would be the same he'd made in high school.

With one eyebrow cocked, David asked, "You wouldn't know anything about a strange little man coming to visit me in a boat that looked just like the one we used to go out in, would you?"

Biff slapped his menu on the table. "Shoot! I owe your wife ten dollars. Remind me never to bet with her again. When did you catch on?"

"Not until last night. I didn't have a clue until I noticed the boat go to another bay house. Who is that guy, anyway?"

Biff waited until the waitress delivered, and sloshed, their coffee. "His name is Dr. Luther Martinson. You'll have to ask CJ for details. She told me someone named Aunt Bea recruited him to unscramble your brain. I'm sitting at home watching an Astros game when two men with badges and guns invite themselves into my living room. Before long, I'm on a conference call with your wife."

David nodded as the plan came into focus. "Whose bay house did Luther go to after he left me?"

Biff's grin beamed with mischief. "A game warden. They

recruited him to keep an eye on you and Luther. We rigged up a device inside my fishing shack. If Luther needed help, all he had to do was press a panic button. The warden would've fired up his boat and been there in no time."

"That explains the emblem."

"Did you sleep well?" asked Biff with a mischievous grin.

David tilted his head and nodded. Revelation struck him like a sledge hammer. "Someone spiked those energy drinks."

Biff chuckled. "What's good for the gander is good for the goose. Another of Aunt Bea's ideas. She kept CJ knocked out and did the same to you. You were on a caffeine-only diet and needed sleep."

Humility mingled with thanksgiving. How many people had been involved in saving David from himself?

The shifting of Biff's gaze toward the door told David the third member of their party had arrived.

"Hello, David," said a man wearing cowboy cut slacks, a white shirt and a badge similar to the one David carried in his pocket.

David stood and looked eye to eye with the lanky man wearing a straw cowboy hat. "Quint Fowler, it's good to see you again. How about some breakfast? Biff's buying. He owes my wife ten dollars."

The ranger cut his eyes toward Biff. "What a coincidence. He owes me for dry cleaning." Quint shifted his gaze to David and pulled out a chair. "Yesterday evening, about nightfall, I met this so-called friend of yours at the dock to pick up Dr. Martinson. I needed to get a report on how you were doing and carry the good doctor to a private airplane. Before I could leave, Biff talked me into helping him load that broken-down excuse for a boat on its trailer. Do you know what he did? Right when I'm lifting the bottom of the motor to lock it in place, Biff pulls out the drain plug. Nasty bayou water mixed with oil and gasoline squirt all over my slacks and boots. And there he is, laughing his fool head off."

David set his face like granite to keep from laughing out loud. "I can't believe he'd make a mistake like that. In all the years I've known him, I've never seen him do anything like that."

The waitress arrived, not only chewing gum, but popping it as she applied ball-point pen to order pad. She retreated to the kitchen and Quint faced David. "I'm sorry I didn't get the second name out of Barcroft."

"You did your best. I'm sure you'll find out who else needs to pay."

"No, David, we'll find out who else did it. I've been instructed to send you copies of everything I have on this mess. And believe me, it's a mess."

David raised his brow in question. "The last I heard I was to stay away from the case."

"The director relented. Right now, we need all the help we can get." The ranger leaned in and whispered, "The sheriff's department, the D.A., the district clerk and a judge are all involved in some real shady goings on. Somehow, everything leads back to your mom and dad."

Shocked, not only by the scope of the potential corruption, but also by Ranger Fowler divulging so much in front of Biff, David didn't respond.

Seeing David's reluctance to talk in front of a civilian, Fowler explained, "Don't worry. Biff's wife works with us. We have her planted in the District Clerk's office. She's been gathering intel."

Biff glowed with pride. "See there, buddy. You're not the only one married to a superhero."

Oval platters arrived, piled high with eggs, bacon, hash browns, and pancakes hanging off one end. The complementary buttermilk biscuits and sausage gravy came as side dishes. The three dug in like they hadn't eaten in a week.

Following the gluttony, Biff belched, looked at his watch, then at David. "Don't you have a wedding to go to?"

David sprang from his seat. "I almost forgot. I've got to get out of here." Two twenty-dollar bills fell to the table. "I still have to drive five hours to Riverview, get cleaned up and make it to Austin by seven. CJ will tan my hide if I miss John and Dotty's wedding.

"Quint, thanks for bringing me up to speed with the case. I'll start reviewing the files when I get home."

David gave a friendly slap to Biff's shoulder. "I'll see you at the reunion, if not sooner."

CHAPTER THIRTEEN

CJ's new one-ton diesel pickup sat outside the barn. Being a bridesmaid, she'd left hours before with Bea and Billy Paul. Sandy's yelps of joy greeted David before the truck came to a stop. "Hello, girl. Did you miss your daddy?" Her tail whipped to-and-fro as she received rubs. "Did you take good care of your momma? It's back to your own bed from here on."

Even though he risked running late, David allowed Sandy to lead him through a deserted construction site. The workers had returned to their homes and families for the weekend. "My goodness girl, look at all the work they've done. The exterior rock work is two thirds finished, the sheet rock is up, taped and floated. They should texture it Monday and be ready to paint by Wednesday or Thursday. What about it, girl, two more weeks?" Sandy sneezed and shook from muzzle to tail. "You're right, closer to three weeks."

To Sandy's barking delight, David ran from the back patio to the barn. He entered the bathroom in the corner of the barn and beamed. CJ had hung his shirt and suit on the shower rod and laid out everything else he needed on the vanity. A folded note dangled from the mirror.

Welcome home, husband. I missed you and love you so much. You probably wasted time looking at the house with Sandy. I told her to keep guard over everything tonight. I've booked a room for us in Austin. I have everything you'll need. You'd better hurry. I'm sure you're running late.

"Sandy, Daddy is out of the dog house. Let's see how quick I can get cleaned up and get to Austin."

Dressed in a black suit with tiny pinstripes, a new white shirt, and handmade black cowboy boots, David slipped on his shoulder holster and felt the familiar comfort of the .45 pressed against his side. He locked the barn and told Sandy to keep guard. She exited through her doggie door and followed him to the new truck.

David patted Sandy's golden head. "Momma and Daddy will be home tomorrow around noon. You be a good girl and guard our home." Sandy disappeared around the corner of the house and performed her first perimeter check.

David pointed the truck toward the interstate for the hour-and-a-half trip. His thoughts drifted back to the briefing he received from Quint Fowler. For the first hour he placed scraps of information into various files in his mind. It would take hard work and time, but the pieces of the puzzle would come together.

When his truck passed the Austin city limits sign, he closed the imaginary file cabinet and allowed his mind to turn to CJ. By the time he reached a packed church parking lot, he could hardly wait to see his beloved Catherine Jo.

He slipped into an open seat just in time. Due to the angle and the pastor's short stature, David couldn't see his face, but the voice sounded eerily familiar. He opened the program an usher had thrust in his hand. It only took a glance.

Reverend Luther Martinson.

David's unplanned chuckle brought a stare from a fellow latecomer. He pushed down an outright laugh and mumbled, "What a conspiracy."

The wedding proceeded without a hitch. The bride glowed, the groom didn't trip over his lines, and CJ sang an amazing solo with a three-piece string accompaniment. David's heart swelled with feelings of indescribable thanksgiving. He also committed to never again keep CJ out of any corner of his life.

As the recessional played and the bridal party made their way down the aisle, David slipped out a back door. He scooted across the lobby and waited, hidden by the main double doors. An insistent pull on her arm brought CJ into his arms. She held him off at arm's length. "Not so fast, Mister Harper. You have some serious apologizing to do."

"You're right. Please forgive me." He looked down. "I know that wasn't much of an apology. And I have a lot of explaining to do. Tonight, I promise."

She reached her arms around him and held tight. "You're a big jerk."

David stepped back from her embrace and grinned. "Guilty as charged, but I ask the judge for her forgiveness."

"Lord, have mercy," said Bea as she approached. "There's nothing like overcoming a crisis, time apart, and going to a wedding to get a man and woman back on track."

CJ hooked her arm in David's. He tried to convey his thanks to Bea, but she shushed him. "Your wife and that preacher did the heavy lifting. Isn't he the best thing since they put toilet paper on a roll?"

Bea scanned the room. "If I can find that handsome husband of mine, we'll head to the reception." She kept looking. "My Lord, have you ever seen the likes of this crowd?" Her eyebrows shot up. "There he is. Billy Paul, get your handsome self over here and shake David's hand. He's home from the sea and looks almost as good as you do."

"Howdy, David." The economy of words and the mist-covered blue eyes spoke volumes.

"Billy Paul, you had to be involved in all this. Thank you."

A nod of the head sufficed for a response. Bea grabbed Billy Paul by the hand. "Come on. It's time to put on our dancin' shoes. There's good food and a fine band waitin' for us at the reception."

David leaned into his wife. "Do we have to go to the reception?"

She tented her hands on her hips. "You still have one foot in the dog house, mister. Besides, Dotty said they went all out."

A smile flashed across David's face. "Let's go. I'm starving."

"By the way, Dr. Martinson wants to talk to us tonight."

CHAPTER FOURTEEN

David and CJ took their turn on the dance floor when the band played a slow waltz. They strode from the hardwood after the first notes of an up-tempo country-rock song. Luther Martinson joined them after finishing the waltz with a woman in her twenties, who would have been quite attractive had it not been for her complexion. The heavy makeup helped, but couldn't hide the telltale scars of severe acne.

"Honey, will you excuse me? I need to have a few words with these good people."

The young woman smiled and unhooked her arm.

Luther lifted a hand in the direction of the door. "Let's find a place where we can talk." The pastor blazed a serpentine trail through tables and guests. He traveled down a hallway and swung open the door to a vacant room lined with books. Leather wingback chairs, sofas and thick area rugs over dark hardwood gave the room the feel of money. The odor of cigars overpowered the scented candles that burned in a rock fireplace. With an outstretched hand, Luther motioned for David and CJ to take a love seat while he sat across from them.

"David, I have a present for you," began Luther, as he handed David a book.

David scanned the cover. The title read, *REVENGE: How to Get Back at People Who Hurt You.*

"You already know most of what's in this book. I tell my story of growing up and everything that happened to me, just like I told you at the bay house."

David interrupted, "I think you left out a few things. The church you lead now is the size of a college basketball arena." David waved a hand and looked around the room. "And I don't think this is the first time you've been to this country club. You're a far cry from the dirty guy lying in the bottom of an old fishing boat saying he wants to end it all."

Luther gave a hand-in-cookie-jar smile. "Desperate times call for desperate measures. I may not have ever been in a dirty little boat before, but I can't tell you how many times I wanted to end my life."

Luther leaned forward. "Everything, including getting kicked out of that church, really happened. By the time they invited me to leave I'd already written most of what you have in your hand. I'd also been called to come to Austin."

David asked, "So you became pastor of that huge church we were in tonight?"

"It wasn't big when I came to Austin. In fact, you could fit the entire congregation inside this room." The master story-teller waited a beat before he resumed his story. "I finished the book you're holding. It started jumping off the bookshelves and eBook sales soared. Before long, people flocked to our church. We had to rent bigger and bigger places to worship. I gave the proceeds from the book back to the church and we started building. Even with all my training, I never realized how many people have such deep-seated anger for things others have done to them. God sent person after person, family after family, to us. They all wanted real, permanent relief from past hurts. Dotty and her daughter Hope joined during my first year."

David looked at the cover of the book again and raised his gaze to Luther. "So, how do you really get back at people who hurt you?"

Luther peered through the lenses of wire-frame glasses. "The ultimate revenge you can take on someone is to forgive them. When you do, you release yourself from the bondage of hate. Healing power is released in ways we cannot imagine."

Luther reached out and touched David's knee. "When did the rage leave you at the bay house?"

"Let's see...it was after I spilled my story. You asked me again why you shouldn't end your life. I reached out and grabbed your cross."

Luther nodded, "The rage left when you went to the cross. At that moment, you started the process of forgiveness."

David lowered his chin. "Process? I feel great. Why do you say I've only started the process of forgiveness?"

The pastor shrugged. "Rage can leave quickly, but anger and offense take much longer. You have an extra burden. You're a policeman working on the case. You'll be tested. You have a long way to go. You haven't even begun to forgive your mother's killers."

David nodded. "I don't know if I'll ever be able to do that."

"Time will help," said Luther. "Start with forgiving someone you know quite well."

David searched his mind and came up blank. "Who's that?"

Luther smiled a smile of hard-earned wisdom. "It's you,

David. You haven't begun to forgive yourself. Your dad ceased to exist in your mind when you had your name changed. I did some checking. You still haven't contacted your father, even though you know he's completely innocent."

David's chin rested on his chest.

"You buried your dad in a concrete tomb with steel bars."

The words stung but David knew they were true.

Luther didn't let up. "Your dad is coming out of prison. He's also being resurrected from the tomb you put him in. Who's going to meet him? Will it be a son racked with guilt and shame, or a son filled with life and joy? Until you forgive yourself, you'll never be the son your dad deserves."

"There's one more thing I don't understand." He looked up at Luther. "Why couldn't I tell CJ about my past?"

"Two reasons," said Luther. "This is going to sting. Are you ready?"

"I'm already stinging. I might as well get it all out of the way."

"Shame and perfectionism." Luther let the words settle. "The shame of being the son of a man who murdered his wife drove you to perfectionism. You couldn't be this new person under your old name, so you reinvented yourself. This new David Harper would be perfect, a man of complete integrity. A man of justice."

"You make me sound like I wanted to be some sort of comic book hero," said David.

"You tried, until you ran into a situation that proved you're a mere mortal. Now you have to forgive yourself for failing to live up to unrealistic expectations."

Silence filled the room.

CJ broke the mood when she proclaimed, "Both of us are going to read your book and have a crash course. There's a woman who needs to forgive her husband. He kept a huge secret from her for years."

Luther reared back his head and laughed without restraint. When he controlled himself, he added, "Did you two see that beautiful young woman dancing with me?"

Dual nods indicated their answer.

"David, you remember, I told you my first wife divorced me and took our daughter?"

"Yeah, I remember."

"She not only moved away with Jo Ann, she tormented me with hints that she was not my daughter and filled Jo Ann's young ears with lies that her daddy didn't love her. Jo Ann found me her first year of college. Bea Stargate helped her. She said she knew I was her father the moment she laid eyes on me. Blood and DNA tests confirmed it. She works with me at the church now. What a sweetheart she is."

David pushed together his eyebrows, "How did she know you were her father?"

Luther pointed to his pock-marked face. "We both have the same crummy complexion."

As they stood to leave David remarked, "I guess I owe Dotty for telling you about me and twisting your arm into going to the coast."

Luther gave his head a wag. "I'd call it a group effort. It started with that lovely woman hanging on your arm. She told a gathering of friends they needed to get to work saving you from yourself. Dotty and Bea Stargate both blurted out my name at the same time as someone who might be sent to intercept you."

David couldn't help but chuckle. "It doesn't surprise me that you know Bea. She's well known for her research and success with depression and suicide prevention."

"I've known Bea for years. Jo Ann's one of her former Honey Bees. Bea took a frightened girl under her wing and paired her with a student with cerebral palsy. They're still best friends."

"Who else had a hand in this?"

Luther grinned. "Let's see, Billy Paul took care of transportation by flying me to and from the coast in his private plane. I had a tight schedule and only had one day I could be away from the church. Your supervisor, Herbert Crow, took care of contacting Quint Fowler. He put the panic button in Biff's bay house and arranged for the game warden to be close by. That gave me a place to clean up for the flight home. I made it just in time for the rehearsal. Finally, there's Biff." He grinned. "Where did you find him? That man has the best-developed sense of humor I've ever seen, even if it is a little twisted. He's turned belching into a strange form of art."

David smiled at the accurate description of his friend. Then, his expression sobered. "I..." David looked at CJ. "That is, we, can't thank you enough for dropping everything and coming to my rescue."

"It didn't take any twisting of my arm. I'm under pressure from my publisher to write a second book. With your permission, I'd like to use my recollections of our time together for a chapter. Of course, I'll change the names."

David and CJ exchanged nods. CJ spoke for both of them, "If it will help others, use anything you need."

David's wrinkled forehead caused Luther to ask, "What is it David? What's on your mind?"

"It's Dad and all the things he'll have to work through. This is asking a lot, but could you work with him after he gets out?"

Luther pulled a letter from his pocket. "David, I've been interested in your father's case for some time. The Lord brought him to my attention through a newspaper article. I've been writing to your father for months. He's agreed to let me use his story for another chapter in the book. I can't let you read it, but yesterday I received this letter from your father."

David's body convulsed when he saw his father's handwriting. He fell onto the love seat, dumbstruck.

CJ sat down and held his hand. She looked up at Luther. "Is he all right?"

Luther nodded. "Ever since high school David's lived in a world where his father didn't exist. This letter is like looking at something written from the grave."

CJ nodded. "When should David go see his father?"

Luther shrugged. "Hard to say. I'd suggest he work through forgiving himself first."

He stood and walked toward the door. Stopping, he turned to face them. "I'll leave you two alone. When you're ready, come back to the party. It's time to celebrate. I'll introduce you to Jo Ann."

CHAPTER FIFTEEN

Cicadas sang their summer song as CJ counted stars while standing at the door to their barn. She squared her shoulders, took in a full breath of country air, and asked, "Have you figured out how to investigate what happened to your dad?"

"Is that coffee fresh?" David walked to the makeshift table.

"Don't change the subject."

David poured a cup and returned to his seat. "I'm not. I'm trying to find words to answer your question." A pause followed. "I need to keep everything at arm's length. I'll study the evidence already gathered and look for things Quint might have missed, or didn't recognize. If I need an interview done, Quint or someone else can do it."

"What is it, David? You look worried."

He nodded. "There's one interview I have to do myself."

"Who's that?"

"I have to see Dad. After all he's been through, he's reluctant to talk to Quint. His lawyers told him not to trust anyone. I can't say I blame them."

CJ reached out her hand and laced her fingers in David's. "Do you think your dad holds the key to who killed your mom?"

"He may. First, I'm looking for why. After I find that out, it should be a clear trail." His voice lowered. "Why would someone want to break into our home and kill Mom? A simple burglary that got out of hand? Could Dad have been working on something worth stealing?"

CJ's eyebrows pushed together. "You never told me about your dad. What's he like? What could he have been working on that someone would want to steal?"

"Dad's a mechanical engineer. He's an inventor and has several patents. He worked for one of the big chemical plants in the area, but he loved to tinker. Always some new gadget."

David looked wistfully into the past. "Dad had a sense of humor as dry as the Sahara. He could tell you a whopper of a story and make you believe it. He once told Biff he invented a special powder that made people invisible and Biff believed him. He took some to school and doused himself with it during English class. Mrs. Wilson caught him with one foot out the door. The powder turned out to be for athlete's foot. Dad put it in a fancy shaker with a made-up chemical compound taped on it. He loved to string people along and wouldn't laugh until they realized they'd been had."

David became more animated. "Dad even joined the liar's club. A bunch of college engineering buddies got together each year and gave awards for some invention or chemical formula that did something miraculous. Of course, none of them worked. He spent months on those things."

"What were some of his inventions?"

"Things like perpetual motion machines that created energy on their own. One year he entered a screen for a porthole on a submarine. He claimed it would let the breeze from the ocean currents in while keeping the water out. He got a second place for that one."

"Good grief, what took first place?"

"A dehydrated water pill. You set it in a glass and it attracted water molecules from the surrounding air. In fifteen minutes, you had a glass of water. I remember seven pages of chemical formulas and explanations of how it worked. The funniest thing was watching people stare at a pill in a glass." David laughed out loud. "I bet those people are still waiting for a drink of water."

Excitement rose in CJ. "I can't wait to meet him. Can I go with you?"

"Yes and no. It's best that I see Dad alone the first time. His attorney wants to be with me to make sure it's legit. We had a hard time convincing him we weren't up to something."

CJ stuck out her bottom lip.

"While I'm with Dad, I have an assignment for you in Brazoria County. This may seem off the subject, and it may not amount to anything, but I need you to help me with something only you can do."

CJ nodded and waited for David to continue.

"There's a jailer I want you to interview. An escaping inmate beat her so bad she had to be hospitalized for a week."

A chilled memory gave her a tingle. "You mean the biker that tried to kill me?"

He nodded. "I've been looking at the reports from the escape. Something doesn't smell right. It's a gut feeling, but I can't shake it."

"How can his escape have anything to do with your mom and dad?"

"It may not, but it's like a loose thread I can't ignore. The woman's name is Kay Weatherby. She refuses to talk to Quint about what happened."

Both looked at the river. "What do you want me to find out?"

"Whatever you can. Were normal procedures followed on the night of the escape? Was there other shady stuff going on in the jail? How did the inmate get out of his cell?"

CJ's eyebrows pinched together. "That information will be old. How will it help you with what's going on now or what happened sixteen years ago? Can't someone besides Quint find out what's going on there?"

A coyote on the other side of the river let out a high-pitched cry. David came on point. CJ repeated her question.

David refocused. "Everyone working at the jail is scared to death of the sheriff. Quint can't get anyone to say a word. I wish we could get one of our people in there."

"Have you tried?"

"Quint tried to plant four different undercover officers as jailers. The sheriff is no dummy. Only one of them made it past the interview process. He lasted one day."

A long minute passed. "Did you check the backgrounds for the plants?" asked CJ.

"They all had good credentials. Clean criminal histories, good references, above adequate education."

"That may be your trouble. Put yourself in the place of a crooked sheriff. You'd want people you could control."

David snapped his fingers. "That's right. He'd be looking for people he had leverage over. It might be the jailer themselves, or even a close relative. What if we run background checks on the jailers and their families? There's no telling what we might find. I'll get a list of all the jailers from Quint and start checking."

CJ spoke through a yawn. "Do you need help? Dotty and John will be back from their honeymoon this weekend. He'll be back to work on Monday. I should have some free time, too."

David's eyes had a twinkle in them. "That would be good. I'm swamped with my caseload." He rubbed his hands together. "Check for criminal backgrounds of the jail staff. Take a look at bank accounts and credit reports. Let's see how many are in deep debt. You'll also need to look for probated or suspended sentences. While you're at it, check pending criminal or civil cases."

"Whoa. Don't forget I have my own job to do." She smiled and took his hand. "Sounds like you're concentrating on money and things dealing with the court."

Releasing her hand, he looped his arm around her shoulder. "You're not only beautiful, you're very smart. After reviewing Quint's file material, I'm looking at four elected officials: the sheriff, the district judge, the district clerk, and the district attorney."

"Why the district clerk?"

"She processes the money for the courts. That includes fines, fees, and bail. When in doubt, follow the money." David gave her a sideways smile. "You might also like to know the district clerk is the judge's daughter. I dated her in high school. She's the one that broke into the city pool with Biff and me."

CJ leaned back. "An old girlfriend? That would be awkward if you have to arrest her."

David either pretended not to hear her or ignored her, lost in thought.

She continued to take in the river and said, "It would help if we had someone planted in the district clerk's office."

He took CJ in his arms. "We do. I understand she's a cute redhead who's married to a scoundrel. Her name is Amy Stewart."

"Biff's wife?"

"Yep. We're scheduled to have dinner with them next Thursday."

"That means next Friday I'll try to meet with Kay Weath-erby, and you'll be with—"

David didn't let her finish. "I'll see my father for the first time in sixteen years."

CHAPTER SIXTEEN

C rushed oyster shells covered the parking lot instead of gravel and crunched underfoot. An oversized clapboard house on telephone poles rose from the ground, looking tired and sunbaked. A weathered stairway led to a screen door with its holes duct taped to keep out most of the mosquitos. Gulf breezes whisked away most of the muddy smell of the bayou that ran along the back of the restaurant.

"You always take me to the nicest places," said CJ.

"Yeah, it's a little rough." David ran his palm over his cheek. "Biff assured me this place has the best seafood around. I guess he and Amy are running late. I can understand why with four kids."

Boards squeaked and the entire stairway wobbled as they ascended. A hand-painted sign on the door read, NO SHIRT, NO SHOES, NO BRA...NO PROBLEM.

CJ raised her eyebrows. "I may have overdressed."

The door moaned its way open at David's tug. "Let's get a glass of iced tea. That five-hour drive left me parched."

Inside, decorated in early neon, the room boasted a dining area of around fifteen tables with plastic table cloths and a small bar. "Nice," muttered CJ. She scanned six men on stools slouched over cobbled-together planks of wood. Each had a long neck beer bottle in front of him. Four picked at labels while two waxed eloquent about something to do with politics. Cigarette smoke curled upwards and headed for an open window.

David tried to make the best of the situation. "You have to admit, this place has character."

"So did London during the black plague."

David's hand found the small of her back and gave a slight of nudge. "I don't see a maître d' to seat us. How about that table by the far windows? It's in the non-smoking section."

CJ spoke in a low tone, trying not to offend the label-peelers. "I think the health department is scared to come in here."

They turned to cross the dining room but stopped dead in their tracks. From the parking lot came the screech of a wild boar followed by, "WOOO...PIG...SOOIE!"

One of the men at the bar raised his head like a bird dog catching a scent. "There's Biff. You fellers think he's got a joke for us today?"

While the bar patrons debated, the steps creaked until the screen door flew open. In walked a petite woman in high heels and a silk dress. Hair the color of raw carrots glistened under the glow of beer signs. Biff guided her across the room. His grin threatened to touch his ears.

He nodded to CJ and David while holding a lone index finger skyward. "Hold on a minute, I have to give these guys a joke. Oh, yeah, this is Amy. Amy, this is David and CJ."

Biff wheeled and walked to the edge of the bar. "Hello, sinners."

The six men on stools each raised their bottles in a salute to Biff's greeting.

"Whatcha' got for us today?" asked a nine-fingered man sitting on the end nearest the door.

Biff spoke loud enough for anyone in the room to hear, if they cared to listen.

"A millionaire got so sick he had to go to the hospital. He wanted this old preacher to come see him. A young preacher went along." Biff walked to the center of the gathering of stool perchers. All six men swiveled to face him. "It looked like the millionaire would die. He says to the old preacher, 'People say you're a man God listens to. If you pray and I live, I'll give you half a million dollars. You'd best get to it. I don't have long.'"

Biff paused and allowed the men to comment on how much they would like that kind of money. The coach-turned-comedian took off his ball cap, stuck it under his arm and folded his hands in prayer. "Well, the old preacher prayed down heaven and sure enough the man got better."

"Yeah, then what happened?" asked a man through his few remaining teeth.

Biff replaced his cap. "The millionaire lived but didn't pay the preacher. After a couple of years, the old preacher died. The younger preacher sees the millionaire at the funeral home looking down into the casket. He wonders why the millionaire never lived up to his word. They leave the service and bury the old saint."

"Uh-huh...then what?"

"Curiosity got the best of the young preacher. He goes to visit the millionaire and asks, 'Why didn't you honor your debt and pay the old preacher what you said you would?'"

"'I did,' said the millionaire. 'I wrote him a check and put it in his coffin. He can cash it any time he wants to.'"

Amid a chorus of laughter, knee slaps, and "That's a good one," Biff rejoined Amy. CJ tried not to laugh, but couldn't help herself.

As they took their seats, Amy leaned into her husband. "Are you sure?"

"Yes. Don't believe that old tale. They'll grow back."

Biff looked at CJ and David to explain. "Amy's concerned about our oldest boy. He played a practical joke on his big sister and is now paying the piper. He called the florist and had flowers sent to a boy she's sweet on. The florist delivered them to church at the Wednesday night youth meeting. The card read 'To Jeremy, with all my love.' He signed it 'Rebecca Stewart' so there couldn't be a mistake about who sent it."

"How embarrassing," sympathized CJ.

Biff nodded. "Last night she had her revenge. That boy can sleep through a hurricane. She took shaving cream, lathered him up and shaved off his eyebrows. Amy's afraid they won't grow back."

David grinned and leaned forward. "Where did Rebecca learn to think like that?"

A freckle-faced waitress, pencil thin, whose eyes reflected intelligence with a glint of hard lessons learned, arrived at their table before Biff could voice his comeback. "Hi, Mr. Biff. Hey, Miss Amy. Where are the kids? I hope they aren't home giving the dog another perm."

Biff leaned back. "Hello, Nancy. You're looking pretty as a picture. The last time I saw you, I thought you swallowed a watermelon seed. How's that little boy?"

"Just fine. He's home with Momma. Probably sucking down formula and dirtying a diaper." Her voice trailed off, and she looked down. "I probably shouldn't be saying that right before y'all eat."

The girl turned to face Biff's wife. "Miss Amy, I wanted to tell you how thankful I am for everything you did for me. If you hadn't given me that baby shower, I'd be in a world of hurt."

Amy let a mother's smile respond.

Biff gave the waitress a surprisingly intense gaze. "You didn't return my phone call. It's time I get you registered for GED testing. I can't get you into college until you get that piece of paper."

"Gee, Mr. Biff, my car broke down and it's going to cost me three hundred dollars to get it running again. I can't do much until I get it fixed."

"Don't worry. You keep on working and good things will happen to you. And speaking of working, why don't you bring us a dozen oysters on the half shell and a tray of mud bugs for appetizers."

"Yes sir. What do y'all want to drink?"

"I'll have a cold beer in a bottle. What about you Amy?"

"Water." She looked at her husband. "I might have a taste of your beer."

"Iced tea for both of us," added David.

CJ looked at Biff and Amy. Had two more different people ever been united in marriage? Slim, demure, prim and proper, Amy looked like something out of a high-end catalogue. Biff, on the other hand, sported a dark tan and coaching attire. He careened from one conversation to the next with anyone who would listen and wore a perpetual smile.

Nancy retreated to the kitchen and CJ asked, "Unwed mother?"

Biff pushed back his hat to reveal an untanned forehead. "Yeah, sweet little girl, and smart as Einstein. But, talk about poor. If it took a hundred dollars to go around the world, her mom couldn't make it to the end of the block."

Biff scooted back his chair and rose. "Amy can tell you more about her. I see someone I need to say hello to."

David and CJ leaned forward to catch Amy's whisper-like voice. She told how they met Nancy, befriended her, and walked with her through her pregnancy and the birth of her son.

CJ doodled numbers on a napkin while David observed. He wagged his head to indicate no. She took her pen and doubled the last number. This earned her a nod of approval.

Nancy appeared at the head of the table and plopped down a dozen oysters in open shells nestled in crushed ice on a plastic platter. Nancy's other hand delivered a beer tray piled high with boiled crawfish.

Biff returned as Nancy placed the crawfish on the table. He wiggled his nose, inhaled once, then again, and one more time. "Ahh, Ahh, Ahh-CHOO." Biff's cupped hand rose toward his face as his head came down. With everyone's gaze fixed on him, he looked in his hand and slurped into his mouth what looked like an elephant-sized ball of snot.

CJ cringed and let out an involuntary "Yuk." David sat calmly and didn't say a word. Amy acted as if nothing had happened. CJ hung her head and muttered, "He got me." She glanced down at the platter and confirmed her suspicions—twelve shells, eleven oysters. The room erupted in laughter. Once again Biff scored with the old raw-oyster-in-the-hand-when- you-sneeze routine.

David, Biff and Amy made quick work of the oysters and crawfish while CJ refused the coercions to try one. "I've never been fond of raw oysters. I'm not sure if I can ever eat one now without seeing Biff sneeze. I'll save my appetite for something really good."

Nancy reappeared with an order pad in hand.

"What's fresh?" asked Biff.

"Red fish and flounder. I'd stay away from the speckled trout. It's a couple days old."

"Perfect, I'll take blackened redfish and Amy will have her usual stuffed flounder."

David added, "Blackened redfish for me, too."

CJ turned to David, "I've never had stuffed flounder before, is it good?"

"You'll love it. I guarantee, or you can have my plate."

With the appetizers cleared and time on their hands, David leaned toward Amy. "I've read all the reports you submitted on the district clerk's office. I'd like to know what you didn't put in the reports."

Amy looked at Biff, grabbed his bottle of beer and downed half of it without blinking.

Biff rocked in his chair with laughter. "That will be enough to get her talking for the rest of the night. She only has a drink once or twice a year, but when she does the words flow."

Amy started slowly in hushed tones. "My background is accounting. Once our last child started to school, I began to look for part-time work. I applied for and landed a job at the district clerk's office. It's only twenty hours a week, which leaves me time for the children."

Amy's cheeks began to flush. She reached up, loosed her hair from its loose chignon, and allowed it to fall. Down it came, hanging almost to her waist. CJ's eyelids opened wide at the sudden transformation.

"We go to church with Quint Fowler. He approached Biff and asked if I might be willing to give him reports on what goes on at work. I met with him and told him I would, and I've notified him of every irregularity I find."

David asked, "Have you found many?"

"Sure. With any job there's always something. From what I can tell at this job, they're honest mistakes that are quickly corrected. The books always balance. That's what I do. I audit all the accounts and make sure the debits and credits line up." Amy pursed her lips, narrowed her eyebrows and looked away.

David tilted his head. "What is it? There's something bothering you."

Amy unbuttoned the topmost button on her dress and

spoke a little louder. "There are some things that leave me scratching my head, and it's always with Judge Rhoades' court. As you know, the district clerk collects all the money for bail and fines. I started noticing the people that go through his court don't use bail bondsmen nearly as often. I'm talking about a real high percentage as compared to other courts."

David nodded, "That means the people are posting bail completely out of their own pocket. That is odd."

"Sometimes it's a lot of money. As long as the people show up for court, they're refunded their bail."

"Tell us how that happens." said CJ.

"After the defendant goes to court, the judge issues the district clerk an order to refund bail. Mrs. Shipley does this herself. She issues the checks and logs the person's name and other pertinent information into the computer as well as a log book. The checks are mailed and the people get their money back. They must be getting their money. If they weren't, they'd raise a fuss. There's been an occasional error, but nothing more than with any of the other courts."

David's eyebrows knitted together. "Do you conduct your audit from the computer records or from the handwritten log?"

"Everything I get is from the computer."

CJ spoke next. "That blank look on my husband's face means he's putting what you told him into various files in his mind."

Amy began to massage the back of Biff's neck. With her other hand she freed the next button down. In a complete change of subject, tales of the exploits of the four Stewart children spilled from Amy and caused a cloud of laughter to cover the table until the food arrived.

CJ eased her fork down after the first bite, closed her eyes, and allowed the taste of fresh flounder and crab stuffing to send her taste buds to seafood heaven. "This place may not pass a health inspection, but this is the most delicious thing I've ever eaten. You three talk. I'll join you after I'm through."

Empty plates, except for fish bones and the aluminum foil that wrapped the baked potatoes, sat in front of the satisfied diners. "What else can I get you?" asked Nancy as she removed the plates.

"That'll do it," replied Biff as he turned his head and squinted slightly. "Nancy, did you swallow another quarter this morning?"

"Huh?"

"You must have. Pennies are coming out on your face."

"Mr. Biff, you're always teasing me about my freckles. My little boy is going to have them, too. I guess you'll be teasing him next." Nancy retreated to the kitchen.

CJ reached in her purse, took out her check book and began to write. She completed the task, tore out the check, and handed it to Amy. "David and I have been intending to give a special offering to honor the baby we lost. We didn't know what to do until we met Nancy. If you two don't mind, we'd like you to take this and help Nancy get her GED. If the baby needs anything, use some for that. We trust you to dole it out as she needs it. Please don't tell her where it came from."

Biff leaned into Amy and looked at the check. He gasped. "Now don't you two try to fool old Biff. That check's about as real as the one inside the casket of the old preacher."

David grinned sheepishly and said, "Biff, you remember how my dad was always inventing things?"

"Yeah. So what?"

"I must have inherited some of Dad's ability. The check is real."

"You're not kidding, are you?" Biff held David's gaze and smiled. "Did you get your dad's gold magnet to work?"

A chuckle preceded an answer. "No, I came up with something on my own. I'm surprised you remember that magnet."

CJ reached in her purse once more and took out a stack of hundred-dollar bills. Six fell to the table. "That should cover the bill and leave enough so Nancy can get her car repaired." She leaned toward Biff. "You really need to stop trying to get one-up on me. You lose every time. By the way, your mouth's open."

David slapped Biff on the back. "You lost that round."

The quartet rose. All but Amy strode toward the door. CJ allowed the men to exit while she looked over her shoulder. Across the room the red-haired woman placed a hand on Nancy's shoulder, handed her a month's worth of tips, and talked to her. CJ turned to leave when the teen slumped into a chair and buried her head in her hands.

Amy descended the rickety stairs and joined the other three in the parking lot. "CJ, will you be able to have lunch with me tomorrow? I get off at twelve-thirty."

"Sure. I have an early meeting, but I'll be finished in plenty of time. Why don't I come by your office and pick you up? I'd like to see where you work." CJ shifted her gaze to her husband and spoke out of one side of her mouth. "Besides, I want to see what David's old girlfriend looks likes before we go to the reunion. Why don't you introduce me? You can use my maiden name, CJ David."

Amy chuckled. "Your maiden name is the same as David's first name? I bet that confused people."

"Constant razzing for nine years. I had no choice but to marry him."

Biff stuck his elbow in David's ribs. "Can you imagine a cat fight between CJ and Charlie?"

David wrapped his arm around his wife's shoulder. "If there is, it won't last long."

On the way back to their hotel, David dimmed his lights to oncoming traffic. He turned to CJ. "What time are you supposed to meet Kay Weatherby?"

"Seven-thirty tomorrow morning at a café in Freeport." She paused. "That is, if she shows. She sounded frightened out of her skin when I called today."

"After what she went through, I can't blame her," said David.

They proceeded on to Lake Jackson. A lot depended on what tomorrow would bring.

CHAPTER SEVENTEEN

CJ slid into a booth and ordered coffee. She kept an eye on the door as she scanned the breakfast crowd. Patrons glanced at their watches and slugged down a last cup of motivation. A line of customers waiting to check out stood at a glass-topped counter stuffed with candies, mints and chewing gum. They were the blue-collar laborers, the worker bees of the area, dressed in jeans and shirts with their company name embroidered over the pocket. They stuck toothpicks in their mouths and received words of thanks from the cashier. A woman wearing a baseball cap and sunglasses walked in against the flow. She stopped, pulled down her dark glasses, and searched the booths. The hunt stopped when she saw the one person that looked out of place.

CJ stood as the stout woman approached. "Kay Weatherby?"

She searched the room with a nervous gaze. "Please, don't say my name." Kay removed her sunglasses, revealing eyes filled with fear.

Order pad in hand, the waitress wove through tables until Kay waved her off.

"Thanks for agreeing to meet me on such short notice," said CJ.

"If it had been anyone but you, Trooper David, I wouldn't have come."

"My name is CJ Harper now. I left the highway patrol not long after the incident with the biker. Six months ago I married, and I'm now the assistant chief of police at Agape Christian University."

Kay leaned forward. "I shouldn't have come, but I had to thank you for what you did. I still have nightmares, but nothing like they were before you killed that monster."

CJ let her nod respond to the last comment. Memories of the night she received a scar on her face and killed the fugitive who put it there came back like a torrent. She looked at a lightning bolt-shaped scar on Kay's forehead. "Is that the only place he used the cell key on you?"

Kay shook her head. "I managed to turn over before I blacked out. He held that key in his fist like a roll of quarters and beat me until I stopped moving. There are a bunch of scars on the back of my head. At least they're covered by hair. What about you?"

CJ touched the corner of her left eye and leaned forward. "Between the makeup and the laugh lines, it's hard to see. Look closely; it starts in front of my ear and goes to the corner of the eye."

"You had a better doctor than I did. I can barely see it."

With a bond formed, CJ eased into her questions. "I understand you're still working at the county jail. Is that right?"

Kay's body stiffened. She shifted her gaze to the street beyond the windows. "Yeah, I'm still there, but not for long."

"Are you planning on a career change?"

"Only twenty more days." Kay shook herself back to the present and stared wide-eyed. Her hand covered her mouth, and she whispered through shaking fingers. "Please, you can't breathe a word of what I just said. If he finds out, somebody'll die. Promise me you won't tell anyone I'm leaving."

CJ reached out and touched Kay's hand. "You need to trust me. Tell me what's going on at the jail."

"I can't tell you. It's too dangerous." She paused long enough to reconsider. "I owe you so much. Maybe after we move from this county, I'll feel safe enough."

CJ released Kay's hand, sat back and allowed a long moment. The tension needed to be diluted with small talk. "I had the best stuffed flounder last night. I envy you living down here with all the fresh seafood."

Kay nodded. "That's something we'll miss, but it's about the only thing."

"Moving away may be just what you need. When I left the highway patrol, I reordered my life. I didn't go far, but the change of job and scenery made all the difference. Are you moving to another state?"

Kay leaned on her elbows and lowered her voice. "Please don't talk so loud, especially about us relocating." She looked around to make sure no one listened. "We're getting out of here. I'm not sure where we'll go or what we'll do, but we can't stay."

Like conspirators in a spy novel, the women drew together, heads only a foot apart. "What type of work will you be looking for? Where would you like to live?" asked CJ.

"Somewhere in Central Texas. It don't matter where, as long as Jim Bo can get a driving job."

"What does he drive?"

"Dump trucks most of the time, but he can drive anything with wheels or tracks." Kay's voice abruptly stopped. "I really need to go. I can't be seen talking to you."

CJ knew she shouldn't press any harder, but couldn't leave without a commitment. "I'll make a deal with you. If you agree to talk to me and my husband three weeks from now, I'll have a job waiting for Jim Bo in Riverview. He'll be driving for the best man he's ever worked for. You can stay with us until we can find you a place to live."

Kay tilted her head sideways. "Who is your husband? Why would you do anything for us?"

"My husband is a state trooper who works with the Texas Rangers. His name is David Harper. I'll explain later why this is so important. It's probably best you don't know too much right now."

CJ pulled a small case from her purse. "Here's my card. Call me if you need anything."

Kay took the card, stared at it, and moaned, "Please tell me life can be good again."

CJ straightened her posture. "Better than you ever dreamed it could be."

Kay kept her head down as she scurried from the café. The waitress returned, refilled CJ's cup and pulled an order pad from her apron. "What will you have this morning?"

"This cup of coffee and one to go." She pulled a ten-dollar bill from her purse. "Keep the change."

Sipping coffee, CJ focused her thoughts on Kay. Paralyzing fear had her by the throat; the kind of fear that kept women from leaving abusive boyfriends or husbands. She'd seen the look too many times. Only a clean break fixed the problem, but that came with risks.

The waitress returned with a cinnamon roll and a coffee to go. "You and that lady look like you both got big problems. This is on the house." She looked around. "Not really. I took it out of the tip."

CJ looked up. "Will it help solve problems?"

The waitress spun to leave. "Can't hurt."

Warm and gooey with buttery cinnamon and sugar, the unexpected treat had a comforting effect. David loved cinnamon rolls. He'd be arriving at the prison farm before long. What a ball of nerves he'd been that morning. She'd get another roll to go.

CHAPTER EIGHTEEN

A right hand extended over an oak desk. David grasped it in a firm grip. "Warden McCade, it's good to meet you."

"And you, Sergeant Harper."

The warden turned to the man on David's right, dressed in a dark suit. "Mr. Rosenberg, always a pleasure."

From the scowl on Mr. Rosenberg's face, David surmised the pleasure was one sided.

The warden looked again at David. "You didn't bring Quint Fowler with you? Isn't he heading up the investigation?"

David nodded. "I'm helping Quint. He has the lead."

The warden took another long look at David and turned his head ever so slightly. "There's quite a resemblance between you and the man you're here to see."

David took a deep breath and exhaled slowly. "There should be. He's my father. If it's all the same to you, keep that under your hat. I don't want trouble because Dad has a cop for a son."

The warden nodded, opened a file in front of him, and

began reading. "The social history indicates Inmate Robert Quisenheimer has a son, and his name is David. He lists your last name as the same as his, but you said your name is Harper."

"I changed my name after Dad came to prison. I wanted a fresh start."

"That makes sense. With your dad set to be released, I don't see any reason why anyone here should know you're his son. I'll inform the regional director, but that's all."

The warden leaned back in his chair. "It's a crying shame what happened to your dad. I'll do what I can to help you." He picked up his phone and punched in a number. "Bring Quisenheimer to my office instead of the regular visiting area."

With the phone hung up, the warden continued. "I'll get lost for a while and let you three have some privacy. I've ordered coffee. Otherwise, you won't be disturbed. There will be an officer down the hall if you need anything."

As the warden's boots echoed away, David turned to attorney Clive Rosenberg. "It's my first time to meet him. Warden McCade seems to be a good man."

The attorney replied with a northeastern accent, "From what I've seen, he's an exception."

David nodded. "I understand this has been an uphill battle for you and Dad."

Rosenberg gave David a hard stare. "Sergeant Harper, I only met you a little while ago. I don't know you and I don't trust you. The Rangers say they're working on the case to find out who killed your mother. So far, the only result I see is a dead inmate—Samuel Barcroft. To me, that's one more failure of the system you're a part of."

The attorney stood and pulled a third chair to the front of the warden's desk. "I'll be frank with you. If it weren't for the substantial sum we received from Mr. Stargate, I wouldn't be in the same room with you. I've been stonewalled by the district attorney and the district judge for years. That's not to mention that worthless excuse for a sheriff. I've never seen such a backward county in my life."

The attorney pointed an index finger. "I'm here to represent Mr. Quisenheimer and get him out of this hell hole as soon as possible. I'm not here to help you assuage your guilt, or anything else you might have up your sleeve. If you ask Bob anything that will harm him or delay his release, I'll end the interview."

David nodded. "Fair enough. I only have one or two questions for Dad concerning what happened. My main reason for coming here is to ask my father to forgive me. I also want to ask if he'll live with me after his release."

Approaching footsteps stilled any further discussion. In the hallway Warden McCade instructed his officer. "There's a plainclothes state trooper and an attorney in my office. I want that door kept shut. You're to stand far enough down the hall that you can't hear. Do you understand?"

"Yes sir."

David faced the window behind the warden's desk and rubbed sweaty palms on his trousers. Before the door clicked shut, Clive Rosenberg spoke. "Thank you, Warden. I'll call the officer when we're finished. Hello, Bob. How are you today?"

"I'm ready to get out of this cheap hotel. I understand I'm to see someone. Didn't Ranger Fowler come today?"

With eyes closed David concentrated on the voice he hadn't heard for half his life. He stood frozen, unable to turn around.

With a thick Boston brogue, the attorney spoke. "Bob, you need to brace yourself for a shock."

David opened his eyes and slowly turned. Words refused to come. Robert Quisenheimer's knees buckled. David stepped forward to make sure his father didn't go to the carpet. He hooked both arms under his father's and held tight. An equally tight grip held David as a graying head rested on his shoulder. Long wordless seconds passed. In time, the men separated to arm's length, only to come back together.

"Dad, before you say anything, please let me ask you to forgive me. I've been a terrible son. I abandoned you."

"Let's sit down. I'm feeling a little wobbly."

David sat in the chair beside his father. "Dad, can you ever forgive me? I abandoned you when you needed me most. And worse, I've stayed gone for sixteen years."

Bob tried to speak but couldn't. He cleared his throat and extended his hand. "I forgive you, son. None of this was your fault." Bob wiped tears from his face.

Wiping his own tears, David looked at his father. "Thank you. I'm grateful for this chance at a fresh start."

Bob put his hand on his son's shoulder and squeezed. "A fresh start. That's what I've been praying for."

A knock on the door interrupted the reunion. It creaked open and an inmate dressed in the pressed white uniform of a trustee brought in a tray of coffee and cookies. He placed them on a table against the wall and left without a word or reaction.

With the door once again closed, David walked to the table. "Dad, do you still take cream and sugar?"

A smile pulled up the corners of his father's mouth. "That's the first time I've been asked what I take in my coffee since they arrested me. Yes, please, cream and sugar." His father's gaze started at David's boots and didn't stop until he'd examined the top of his head. "Look at you. You got those final two inches of growth. I told June you hadn't stopped growing."

David's hand shook at the mention of his mother's name.

"Dad, after a while I need to ask you a question or two." He glanced at Clive Rosenberg to see his reaction, then refocused on his father. "But first, I want to ask if you'll consider coming to live with me and my wife after you're released."

Bob folded his hand around David's when he received the cup.

"Is Catherine all right with me coming?"

David's eyebrows shot up. "How do you know her name?"

"I had no idea where you were all these years, but Luther Martinson brought me up to speed. He's quite a man. Whenever I get to feeling sorry for myself, I get out his book." With a washboard brow Bob asked, "Are you sure I won't be intruding on you and Catherine? I understand you've only been married a short time."

David leaned toward his father, "It's a good thing my wife isn't here. There's no telling what she'd do to you."

Bob grinned. "Sounds like you married a woman like your mother. A little grit in her, huh?"

"Sweet as spun sugar, but you better hide the rolling pin if she gets mad."

The elder man's eyes widened. "I understand she grew up on a farm. Is she really a lieutenant at Agape Christian University?"

"Assistant Chief. She received a promotion."

Bob lowered his voice. "I also heard you lost a baby. I'm so sorry. I should have been there for you."

David hung his head. "It was me who wasn't there for you."

Bob reached and gripped David's forearm. "Son, what's done is done. You faced an impossible situation and did what you had to do to protect yourself."

David gazed into eyes much like his own. "All right, Dad. A fresh start for both of us. I'm ready to get you home and kill the fatted calf."

David's father tilted his head back. "Ah, a thick steak with all the trimmings; I can't wait. If I never eat beans and corn-bread again, that would be fine with me."

Clive Rosenberg interrupted. "And speaking of getting you out of here, there are some things I need to cover. The judge finally set a date for your hearing. It's September 24th."

David jerked to attention. "Why so long? The appeals court has already instructed the judge what to do."

The attorney nodded. "Now you get a glimpse of what I've been up against. The district attorney and the district judge have blocked or delayed us every step of the way. The twenty-fourth is the last day the judge can put this off. It's almost as if he has a personal vendetta against your father. Even with DNA tests, we had to go to the court of criminal appeals to get satisfaction. It didn't matter that the proof stared him in the face. The DA is just as bad. He still maintains your father is guilty."

David tapped his lips with an index finger for a few seconds. "Is there any way the judge can order Dad to stay locked up?"

"That's the same question that me and a room full of attorneys and law professors have asked. The answer is no. No, that is, on this charge. The appeals court's ruling is exceptionally firm."

David stood and paced. "You said no on this charge. Are there other charges?"

"There's nothing pending, and since your father has no other criminal history, there can't be anything from the past."

The attorney changed the subject. "Sergeant Harper, you said you had questions for your father. I don't want to rush this reunion, but I have other things I must attend to."

"Sure, I understand." David reached for a manila folder beside his chair and opened it.

"Dad, I need you to look at this. It's an inventory of your office. Study it and let me know if—"

"Just a minute," interrupted the attorney. "Let me see that."

David handed a stack of papers to the man on the other side of his father.

"Where did you get this?"

"Quint Fowler gave it to me. He got it from the evidence file in the district attorney's office. Why? What's wrong?"

"What's wrong?" The question had more than a touch of sarcasm. "Nothing, except we received two of these pages and not the third." He stood and paced. His volume increased. "The appeals court instructed the district attorney to turn over everything pertaining to this case. In your father's original trial, the defense received nothing of value in discovery. Then we got involved and the appeal process started. At first we received redacted copies of documents from witnesses. Then we received only partial field notes from investigators. It's been like finding pages of a book scattered along a highway. The only reason we were able to find the two knives is because they wound up in a box of evidence that belonged to another defendant. Their lawyer saw what they were and called Quint Fowler. Otherwise, they never would've seen the light of day."

David sat shaking his head. "You keep that list. If I need another, I'll get it from Quint."

The attorney straightened his tie, took a deep breath and sat down. "At least this will help the state attorney general when he goes after the judge and the current DA. It's one more thing against them."

The attorney couldn't be blamed for his outburst, but David needed to focus on getting to the bottom of the original crimes. "Dad, when you can, review the list. See if you can remember everything in your office."

"I've seen all but the last page. I should be able to tell you what's missing. Here, let me see it." He took the page and focused through black-framed glasses. "As best I remember, there are only three things in the office that haven't been accounted for. There's my slide rule. That's one. Uh-huh, the bust of Da Vinci on my bookcase. I forgot about Leonardo. That's two." Bob's eyebrows knitted together. "Where's the paperwork for the gold magnet? It's not on this list. I had it typed and ready to go to the liar's club."

Clive Rosenberg threw up his hands. "See what I mean, David? That's the way this case has gone. When you're confident you have everything, something else pops up."

David stood and looked out the window. "I wonder if those particular items are important."

Bob broke in. "I'm sure the slide rule and bust burned in the fire, but if you need the plans for the gold magnet, I made a copy. They should still be around."

"Dad, the house burned to the ground while you were waiting to go to trial."

The elder version of David grinned. "I hid them in a safe place."

Both the lawyer and David asked at the same time. "Where?"

"First, let me tell you why I hid them. It has to do with the rules of the Liar's Club. Each contestant received up to one hundred points for the most outlandish but believable invention. You could earn ten bonus points if you fooled the group on what you did with your copy of the plans to keep them safe. The year before, I didn't come close. I told them I put the plans up the trunk of a stuffed elephant in my den. They knew I'd never hunted elephants. Have you ever heard such a lousy lie?"

The right heel of David's boot pulsated up and down.

"Keep your shirt on, son. I'm getting there. You should

still have that old civil war muzzle-loading rifle. I kept it at Uncle Ray's gun shop."

"Yes sir, I have it. I wouldn't trade it for anything. You gave it to me on my sixteenth birthday. I'm putting it over the fireplace of our new home."

"The plans are down the barrel, rolled tight."

David turned to Clive. "I'll send you copies as soon as I get home."

The attorney asked David's father, "How many pages?"

"Seven. The rules called for a maximum of seven pages."

Attorney Rosenberg turned to David, "I'll expect to receive copies of all seven pages."

"You'll get everything. I give you my word."

Clive's nod indicated he agreed with the arrangement. "That still leaves the plans that were taken off the desk. Where are those?"

David looked out the window again. "I don't know, but I bet whoever has them will wish they'd never seen them."

Clive gave a short tutorial on what to expect in the upcoming court proceedings. David and Bob exchanged final hugs and last-minute talk of times to come. The waiting officer answered David's summons to retrieve the soon-to-be free man and take him to his cell.

"Dad," said David as an afterthought. "Can you make me a list of everyone that knew about your gold magnet and mail it to me?"

"No problem, son. I have plenty of time."

WARDEN MCCADE CAUGHT David and the attorney in the parking lot. "Mr. Rosenberg, do you mind if I have a minute with Sergeant Harper? Thanks."

David slumped in the seat of the warden's vehicle while

the lawyer cranked his car and pointed it toward the entrance.

The warden alternated his gaze between inmates working in a distant field and David. "I assure you, your dad won't be harmed while he's here. I received a call from the director's office the day after the inmate died at the Clemens Unit. The big boss and the regional director told me if anything happened to your father, I'd need to find a new job.

"As soon as I got back to the unit, I checked with my snitches. Sure enough, a hit was planned." The warden focused on David. "We caught the one involved. He had a shank on him when we intercepted him heading to the library where your dad is assigned to work. Of course, he denied everything, but the folks in Huntsville slapped him on the next chain bus headed to West Texas. He's in a nice secluded cell outside Abilene. Since then I haven't received a new inmate who fell from or ever lived in Brazoria County."

"What about the inmates already here? There must be plenty from this area."

"Anyone that ever appeared before Judge Rhoades has been transferred. There weren't that many."

David nodded. "Doesn't that still leave some from this county?"

The warden gave a sideways smile. "Threats work two ways. The word is out that if anything happens to Inmate Robert Quisenheimer, there'll be unpleasant consequences." His voice trailed off and started again. "Let's just say accidents happen in prison. I have the biggest, baddest convicts you've ever seen watching over your dad. There's one in front, one behind and one on each side of him everywhere he goes. And the biggest of all is his cell mate."

"Thanks, Warden. That takes a load off my mind."

"The least I could do for an innocent man." He grinned. "Besides, I'd like to keep my job a while longer."

David turned the key in his vehicle. His mind shifted to CJ and her sleuthing at the county clerk's office. What would she and Amy discover? He chuckled. What would CJ think about his old flame? The last time he saw her, she was one hot surfer-girl.

CHAPTER NINETEEN

"Yes? Can I help you?" The voice came from behind a higher than average counter.

"I'm here to see Amy Stewart. She's expecting me."

The woman's rosy cheeks bobbed up and down. "Amy told me to expect you." A pudgy hand pointed to CJ's right. "If you'll come to the door at the end of the counter, I'll take you to her."

The two women wove their way through a maze of desks until they reached a closet-sized office with glass windows on three sides. Next to Amy's office sat a much larger office enclosed in glass on three sides. A wall of bookcases overlooked a rather untidy standard-issue desk.

"Amy, here's the lady you told me to expect."

Amy raised her gaze from the computer screen. "Thanks, Dorothy. CJ, come on in. Please shut the door behind you. I'm almost ready. Give me a couple of minutes."

CJ remained standing as Amy's slender fingers flew over the numerical ten-key on her computer keyboard. She scanned computer print outs as she worked without words. The office shared a common glass wall with the larger one to

CJ's right. A woman worked with her head down. "Is that her?"

Amy didn't look up or give anything away by her tone. "Yep. Mrs. Charlene Rhodes-Shipley."

Dressed in a dark tailored suit, Charlene's fingers glittered with rings. Unusually blond collar-length hair glowed under florescent office lights. With head down, a pronounced double chin wiggled when she moved her head. Mutilated newspaper remains cascaded over the edge of the wastepaper basket. A black ledger lay closed on her desk.

By narrowing her eyes and taking a step toward the glass, CJ managed to make out a smiling couple in a photo. Encased in a silver frame and sitting at an angle by the computer screen, the subjects looked to be teens.

CJ took in a deep breath. "Does Charlene have any children?"

Amy kept her head down. "No kids."

Taking another step toward the glass, CJ ignored the risk of being caught staring. She had to know, and then she wished she hadn't looked. Two surfboards stood straight up in the sand, a backdrop for the photo. The girl, a teen with hair the color of pale honey, wore a two-piece that accentuated her assets to the fullest. She faced the camera, flashing a carefree smile set in a flawless face. She clutched the muscular arm of a boy racing toward manhood.

CJ glanced away, but only for a half second. An adolescent version of her husband looked down at the girl, his gaze locked and his eyes speaking things she thought only she had heard.

"There," said Amy. "All finished. Do you want to go next door and meet Mrs. Shipley?"

CJ shifted her gaze to the woman in the adjoining office. Charlene absentmindedly retrieved a Hershey Kiss and freed it from its foil covering. The Kiss popped in her mouth while the wrapper joined a pile by the ledger.

The county clerk must have felt the stare. Up came her head and the two women exchanged cordial, yet quick, nods of greeting.

"No, Amy. I've seen all I need to see. I'll let David introduce me to Charlene at the reunion. I doubt she'll recognize me. I wore jeans and pulled my hair back in a ponytail on purpose today. Besides, she looks absorbed in what she's doing."

CJ didn't know what she expected Charlene to look like, but this wasn't it. She also didn't expect the old flame to still be burning. "Let's get some lunch. Is there something close?"

"There's a café across the street with good hamburgers and a nice salad bar."

"Perfect. I'll see if David can meet us." CJ punched a text message into her phone as they walked.

Waiting for you, the text read.

CJ shook her head. "David's already there. If there's a decent cheeseburger in town, he'll find it."

The booth David chose overlooked the street and allowed CJ an unimpressive view.

David's smile beamed. "What a lucky man I am. I get to share lunch with two beautiful women."

Amy didn't respond but CJ grabbed a hug. "Mr. Harper, you're in a good mood. Can I assume you had a nice visit?"

"A few more wrinkles and some gray hair, but otherwise, Dad's in great shape."

"Is he going to come live with us?"

David smiled a crooked smile. "He said he wanted to, but I told him you didn't like the idea."

"David Harper, you've been spending entirely too much time with Amy's husband. Tell me, when is he getting out?

We have furniture to buy and sheets and blankets and dishes and who knows what else."

"Slow down. He's not getting out until the twenty-fourth of September. There's plenty of time."

CJ's shoulders sagged. "Late September? Why so long?" CJ noticed Amy as her head nodded. "What is it, Amy? Does Judge Rhoades always delay things?"

"Not with all cases, but more than the other judges. It's not my area of expertise, but I've heard some rumors."

"Yes?" asked David.

Amy pushed her head a quarter of the way across the table. "It's something about revocation of probation cases. I'm not sure what they're talking about. It has to do with the judge not reducing a sentence when probation is revoked and delaying the hearing as long as possible. It doesn't apply in all cases."

David pulled his eyebrows together. "Can you get us a list of everyone who's posted bail without a bail bondsman for the last ten years?"

She nodded. "Do you want me to give it to Quint Fowler?"

"That's right. I'm afraid we're going to leave him with a lot of homework."

David patted CJ's leg under the table as he swiveled his head. "Did you get to meet Charlie?"

CJ delayed by taking a drink of water. She had to remind herself David had buried his past and that included Charlene. Or did it? "I got a good look at her. That was enough."

CJ turned and addressed the waitress. "I'll have the salad bar and this man playing with my leg will have a cheeseburger with jalapenos and French fries."

The waitress chuckled and asked, "And you, Amy?"

"Salad bar, please."

David brought his hand to the table, ripped open packets

of sugar and stirred their contents into a glass of iced tea. "You didn't talk to Charlie or peek in her office?"

"I saw through the window. From my angle, I saw everything on her desk, and I also saw her computer screen."

Amy interrupted. "It's Friday so you should have seen the written ledger she keeps of all the people who pay cash for bail."

David asked, "What do you use to balance the books?"

"Only the computer print-out. The ledger is her back-up in case the system goes down or is hacked."

"What else was on the desk?" asked David.

"I watched her for a little while," said CJ. "She was cutting articles from newspapers."

David stopped her. "Did you say newspaper, or newspapers?"

"Plural."

"Anything else?"

"Normal stuff. A stapler, calculator, note pads, a bowl of chocolates and a diet soda."

"No pictures?"

The question hung in the air. She crossed her fingers under the table. "Nothing of importance."

The restaurant filled, mostly with women wearing business casual. Amy scooted toward the edge of the booth. "We'd better get to the salad bar before the herd."

"Good thinking," said David. "We still need to meet with Quint and drive home."

CJ walked with Amy while David stayed in the booth. "Thanks for not saying anything about the photo on Charlene's desk."

"That secret's safe with me."

CHAPTER TWENTY

A yellow blur barked an excited welcome home to David's SUV. "There's our girl. She's sure happy to see us," said CJ.

She opened her door and received paws in her lap and wet kisses aimed at her cheek. "Hello, Sandy. Let Momma out and I'll give you a proper rub." Starting at the ears, fingers scratched back and forth down both sides of the rib cage. "Go see Daddy and get some love from him." Sandy obeyed and calmed her shaking body only after accepting a second round of strokes.

"Do you want me to unpack while you open the gun safe and retrieve your dad's plans?" asked CJ.

"If you don't mind."

CJ wrestled a lone suitcase and some hanging clothes into the trailer while David hurried to a trio of substantial gun safes in the corner of the barn. He set up a folding table, retrieved the plans from the muzzle-loading barrel and attempted to straighten a sixteen-year curl from the pages.

CJ stepped down from their temporary home carrying an

armload of dirty clothes to the washer, where she dumped them into a plastic basket.

"That's the plans for the infamous gold magnet?" CJ placed a hand on David's shoulder. "I'm not sure I can focus on this tonight. Why don't you tell me what I'm looking at?"

"Drag up a chair."

CJ pulled a folding chair close to the table and yawned.

David asked, "Do you want coffee?"

"No thanks. I had no idea we would stay so long with Quint. It's way past my bedtime. I'm planning to do some work on the tractor in the morning, so don't be surprised if I disappear in a few minutes."

David retrieved a handful of wrenches and anchored the plans. "I'll give you an overview. Page one is a synopsis of the invention. It tells in general terms what the magnet can and can't do." He flipped a page. "Page two is a listing of all the different alloys used to make up the magnet. It's mainly a lot of metallurgical compounds, their proportions and how they're bonded together." He gazed at several more sheets. "Pages three through five tell how the magnet attracts even ultra-fine gold particles in running water. It's a lot of technical mumbo-jumbo. It says on page five that it can also pick up nuggets in fresh and salt water. On page six there's a description of a sample mining operation. It lists everything from acquiring a gold-bearing stream in Alaska to assaying the gold and selling it. This is interesting. Dad even tells you how to bring raw gold back into the lower forty-eight and sell it. The last page is a spread sheet of projected profits from a magnet the size of a small refrigerator."

CJ rose and placed a hand on David's shoulder. "No wonder they called it the liar's club. You stay up and study. I'm bushed."

Sandy reached out with her front legs, stretching. CJ

looked down at her. "Are you coming with Momma? No? All right, I'll see you two tomorrow."

David spoke without lifting his head. "Are you going to thank Bea and Billy Paul tomorrow for making sure the wheels of justice stayed lubricated with money?"

CJ spoke through her yawn. "I'll talk to Bea sometime tomorrow. In the morning, I'll be clearing my mind by bush-hogging pastures."

"Okay. I'll be working on the case." He looked up. "By the way, I jabbered on so much about Dad, I didn't give you a chance to say anything about your meeting with Kay Weatherby."

After an open-mouthed yawn CJ said, "I'll give you the CliffsNotes...she was too scared to tell me anything useful." She called Sandy. "See you in the morning."

CHAPTER TWENTY-ONE

CJ stood in her new master bathroom and scrubbed off a little makeup and a lot of dust from the ride home from Bea and Billy Paul's house. The new ATV David bought for his father sure was fun to drive. She stepped into the bedroom and couldn't help but smile at the new mattress and box springs, the first arrivals of their bedroom set. What the home lacked in furniture and furnishings, it made up for in room. She still had a few weeks to feather her nest before David's father arrived.

The ring of her cell phone brought her gaze down to a number she didn't recognize.

"Hello—"

A panic-laced voice interrupted. "You have to help us! He's going to arrest Jim Bo. He can't go back to jail. He can't." Gasps for air halted any further explanation.

CJ took long strides as she exited the bathroom, crossed the bedroom, and made for the back door. As she walked, she asked, "Kay? Kay Weatherby? Is that you?"

"Please help us. We don't know what to do. I saw it tonight on his calendar."

CJ burst out the back door, causing David to spring to his feet.

"Hold on, Kay, I'm putting you on speaker phone. My husband is with me." CJ kept talking. "Kay, do exactly as I say. Take a deep breath and release it slowly. Good. Now, do it again, then tell us what's going on."

After the repeated sound of a deep inhale and slow exhale, Kay spoke. "I had thirty minutes left on my shift tonight. The sergeant gave me his keys and sent me to the sheriff's office to get a report. He said he needed to add something to it." Kay took another deep breath and let it ease out. "That's when I saw it written on the sheriff's calendar." The deep breaths temporarily stemmed the flow of tears before they came back with a vengeance.

"It's all right. Take your time," said David.

Kay struggled to speak through short gasps. "The sheriff has a big desk calendar. He makes little notes on the days when he needs to do something important. When I lifted the report, I saw it."

CJ had to wait until another round of sobs subsided. "Kay, what did you see?"

"P U J B W," said Kay before she succumbed again to sobs.

CJ waited in silence until Kay calmed herself.

"Jim Bo is supposed to be off paper on the tenth. On his calendar, the sheriff had written PUJBW on September 7. Only a week and a half left on probation and now he's going back to jail."

David spoke. "Kay, those letters mean Pick Up Jim Bo Weatherby, don't they?"

"Yes. What are we going to do?" Another round of sobbing filled the air space.

David didn't answer. "Today is the fifth. We still have time. We need to get you and Jim Bo out of there. Don't call in to work, either of you. Don't do anything except pack enough clothes for a week. As soon as I hang up, I'm calling a Texas Ranger. He'll call you back tonight and tell you when he'll pick you up. It'll be before dawn. I'll meet you tomorrow someplace outside of Brazoria County."

"But Jim Bo can't leave the county without violating his probation."

"He can if he's in our custody. Officially, we'll be detaining both of you as material witnesses."

CJ re-entered the conversation. "Kay, you're going to have to trust us. It's the only way to break the hold they have over you."

"All right," said Kay in a halting voice. "If you say so, we'll do it."

A silent phone rested in CJ's hand. "My heart's beating like a drum."

David passed CJ on his way inside. "It looks like I'm taking a trip tomorrow morning. I'd better get some sleep."

"DAVID, you have two of the most frightened people I've ever seen inside that truck stop." Quint Fowler's SUV sat beside David's. The lawmen got to work transferring suitcases and travel bags. "I hope you can get more out of them than I did. They wouldn't open their mouths until we crossed the county line. Kay'll be disappointed CJ didn't come. I'm really concerned about her. She's not far from slipping off into the deep end."

David nodded. "I'll make sure a professional sees Kay as soon as we get home. If anyone can peel her off the ceiling, this woman can."

David reached for a bag labeled toys. He raised an eyebrow. "Is this what I think it is?"

Quint tipped his Stetson to rest further back on his head. "You didn't tell me to expect an extra passenger."

"How old?"

"Four months. I'm guessing he has colic. I don't envy you on the ride home."

"Thanks. By the way, did you get the cameras set?"

The lanky ranger closed the back door of his SUV after he handed over the last bag. "All set. We got there about four o'clock. We were in and out in thirty minutes."

"Did anyone see you?" asked David.

"No one that counts. I had Highway Patrol units watch both ends of the road they live on. Nobody came down the street. None of the neighbors had lights on yet. I had them out well before first light."

"Thanks, Quint. I'll call CJ and tell her about the extra guest. Are they ready to go?"

Quint motioned for the trio to come outside. They pushed open the door and walked to where Quint and David waited. The man stood about six feet two and pushed the scales to two-hundred and seventy pounds. A hand the size of a salad plate held firm to Kay. In her arms she cradled a squirming baby wrapped in a receiving blanket.

"I'll get the car seat while you introduce yourselves," said Quint.

With brief introductions concluded, David started the engine to get the air conditioner cooling as the family settled themselves. He closed the rear door for Kay and turned a last time to Quint. "I hope those lists I've been sending you are helping."

Quint returned his hat to its original position. "Keep 'em coming. As soon as your dad is free, those people will be the first ones we take in for questioning. Did you hear the director has asked the state attorney general for a special prosecutor to handle this once we gather enough evidence?"

"No, but that's the smart thing to do. I'm working on another angle or two. Dotty Lewis is going to help us with one of them. I'll run it by you first and we may have to get permission from your senior captain."

Quint issued a smile. "This is beginning to sound like fun. Dotty can make people stand up and take notice."

"I'll be back for the reunion and Dad's court date. Let's meet up then and go over everything."

Quint extended his hand. "Send me an e-mail and tell me when and where. Good luck with that crying baby."

Before David settled in for a noisy four-hour drive, he pulled out his phone and hit CJ's number. "Hi, honey, has your mom left yet?"

"They left a few minutes ago. Did you get Kay and Jim Bo?"

"They're in the car waiting on me. Listen, I need you to get Bea and tell her she has a customer."

"Is Kay all right?"

"Quint's concerned. Can Bea see her today?"

"I'll call and find out. As far as I know, she doesn't have anything planned other than her morning classes. Is that a baby crying?"

"You need some lessons on being a detective. You didn't tell me a baby came with Kay and Jim Bo."

CJ went silent. A baby would arrive at their farm in a matter of hours. David sensed her pain.

"Will you be all right with the new arrangement? If not, I can—"

"I'll be fine. How old is the baby?"

"Four months. With colic."

"Oh, my. You have to travel four and a half hours with a crying baby? That calls for double hazardous duty pay."

"See you when I get there."

Thirty minutes later David's phone vibrated in his pocket. He mashed it hard against his ear.

"CJ, is that you? You'll have to speak up. It's a little noisy in here."

"I said Bea will be here when you arrive. She recommends we put Kay and Jim Bo in the trailer."

David raised his voice above the screams. "Ok. I'm making better time than normal. Only three more hours."

Fifteen minutes from arriving home, David turned to Jim Bo. "It sounds like little Bo finally wore himself out."

"Yep."

David looked out the driver's window and smiled. Billy Paul and Jim Bo were two of a kind. They'd get along just fine.

Bea made a quick assessment and returned to the back porch. "CJ, what this family needs more than anything is to feel safe. Peace and quiet is going to go a long way toward that. Take them food, but leave them alone for at least twenty-four hours. Give Kay this medicine for the baby." Bea rummaged in her purse and retrieved a bottle. "This will take the gas off his stomach. Tell them to lock the barn at sundown. That'll put two walls between them and what has them so afraid."

Bea climbed into her ATV, but stopped before she turned the key. "It looked like Sandy took to Kay and Jim Bo right off. See if you can get her to stay in the barn tonight. A guard dog will give them extra peace of mind."

CJ settled her guests in the recently-vacated travel trailer. She told them David and Sandy were there for them and instructed Sandy to stay close. With nothing more to be done, she climbed into her truck and headed to town for something to feed her guests.

"I hope Kay and Jim Bo like fried chicken. How do people work a full day and then come home and cook a big meal? One thing I'm not is a cook. I think I missed that gene." CJ shrugged. "I am what I am, Lord. Just the way you made me."

The supercharger on her diesel truck came to life after she hit the Farm-to-Market blacktop road. Driving fast had become a way of life. She took in a field of stubby corn stalks, the remnants of a bountiful harvest. Somehow her mind linked the harvest to retrieving David's father. The next few days with Kay and Jim Bo would be a sort of harvest, an important harvest. They'd be harvesting information.

CHAPTER TWENTY-TWO

The next afternoon CJ crossed the kitchen and placed two white plastic sacks on the granite countertops. She hurried to the bedroom and put on yesterday's blue jean shorts and an ACU T-shirt. When she opened the back door, she saw David walking toward her. "You're home early," she said.

"Things are heating up," said David. "I need to spend time with Kay and Jim Bo tonight. Besides, I wanted to see the progress on the pool. It looks good. They got more done than I expected."

"I'm on my way to check on our guests. I'll tell them you need to talk with them after supper." CJ's flip-flops stayed on the well-worn path between the house and barn to avoid grass burs.

Kay sat in a lawn chair inside the door, while the baby's play pen occupied floor space to her right. Little Bo lay on his back cooing and sucking a wet fist. Sandy guarded the play pen's right flank. She raised her head and wagged her tail as CJ's approached, but didn't leave her post.

"My goodness, he's precious. There's no way this child is only four months old. He's half grown."

A smile pulled up the corners of Kay's mouth. "You can pick him up if you want to."

CJ both dreaded and looked forward to this moment. How would she react to a young life in her arms? Steeling herself, she lifted the infant. He weighed more than expected. "You don't miss many meals, do you Bo? He looks like he's feeling better today. Any more colic?"

"That medicine did the trick. Bea and Billy Paul stopped by after lunch and brought us another bottle. It's amazing. He's only been here a day, and he's happy as a pig in slop."

CJ smiled, lowered Bo back into his playpen, and jangled a set of bright-colored plastic keys over him. He reached out with a pudgy hand, grasped the keys, and moved them to his mouth. Bowed stubby legs kicked for joy.

CJ knew she'd passed a test of sorts. Her heart still ached, but the acute pain subsided with each passing day. She had her husband back, and David's father would soon join them. The irony of losing a baby while gaining a father-in-law struck her.

CJ retrieved a chair and sat where she could see Kay and Bo. "Where's Jim Bo?"

Kay's face brightened. "Working."

"He's working? Where?"

Kay leaned toward CJ. "Like I said, Bea and Billy Paul stopped by. You should have seen Billy Paul and Jim Bo."

"What happened?" CJ leaned forward with anticipation.

"Bea and I started talking. Before you could say lickety-split, I jabbered on like I'd known her all my life. We rattled back and forth for fifteen minutes before taking hardly a breath. Just talk. Nothing important. Mainly about little Bo. When we finally slowed down, Billy Paul looks at Jim Bo and says, 'Howdy.'"

Kay stood and played both roles by shifting from side to side and changing her voice to mimic the two men.

"'Howdy,'" says Jim Bo."

"'You drive a truck?'"

"'Yep.'"

"'Operate a dozer?'"

"'Yep.'"

"'Ready to work?'"

"'When?'"

"'Now. I need a stock tank dug. Dozer's filled up and waitin'.'"

Kay settled herself in her chair. "Neither one said another word. They loaded up in Billy Paul's truck and left me and Bea here with our faces hanging out. Bea borrowed your ATV to get home. She said she'll bring it back when they come for supper."

CJ's head dipped and returned. "It sounds like Jim Bo and Billy Paul are kindred spirits."

Kay looked toward the river. Worry lines again creased her forehead. "I hope it lasts."

Instead of responding to Kay's doubt, CJ relaxed in her chair and allowed the end-of-summer stillness to bring in its own measure of peace. Only small talk and baby gurgles broke the silence. The sound of an approaching pickup truck and an ATV broke the spell of the river.

Kay rose from her chair and rolled her hands together as Jim Bo's footsteps approached. Seeing his quiet grin and the peace on his face, she threw herself into her husband's arms.

"Thank you, Lord. Thank you, Lord. Thank you, Lord," said Kay in a low refrain.

CJ rose and left the family to celebrate Jim Bo's first day of work for Stargate Enterprises. Sandy took a respite from her guard duties and followed her mother to the house, with one small detour to water the grass.

The ATV pulled into the shade and Bea strode toward the new home. She made it to the back-porch swing and plopped down as CJ approached from the barn. "Have a seat here by me on this porch swing. This is the best place I ever saw for watching that old river wander by."

"I'll be right back. Let me get us a glass of iced tea." CJ opened the back door and passed the island that separated the kitchen from the breakfast nook. David awaited her arrival with glasses poured and a long kiss.

He spoke in a husky voice. "I put the hot things in the oven to stay warm and the cold dishes in the refrigerator. I guess you had other things on your mind when you got home."

CJ pressed her head to her husband's chest and pulled tight against him. "Who cares about food?"

"There you go again, starting something I can't finish."

A coy smile, a turned head, and raised eyebrows sufficed for *later*.

David resumed his kitchen duties by handing CJ two glasses of refreshment. "Take these to Bea and Billy Paul. I heard him pull up. I'll bring yours out to you."

In the lengthening shadows of evening, David lowered himself onto new lawn furniture. His gaze shifted from the barn to Billy Paul. "How did Jim Bo work out on the dozer today?"

"Fine and dandy. One of the best operators I've run across in quite a spell."

"Does he have a drinking problem? He's on probation for DWI."

Billy Paul tilted his green John Deere baseball cap back on his head. "No problem. I asked him straight out. He told me he ain't had a drop since he got serious about Kay. She told him right quick that it would be her or a bottle. He couldn't have both. I believe him."

Bea broke in. "Sugar doodle, do you have enough work for him?"

"There's another stock tank to dig after this one and then there's that patch of scrub cedar I've been meaning to clear. That's at least four week's work. After that he can drive a dump truck or run a front-end loader at the rock quarry. Don't matter to me which one."

CJ nodded. "That should be plenty of time for us to help them find them a place to live."

A familiar car pulled into the driveway. Dotty slid out of the driver's seat.

"Where's the rest of your tribe?" asked Bea.

"Meet-and-greet night at the girls' school," replied Dotty. "John's getting them ready. I'll join them there."

The back porch continued to fill with the arrival of Kay and a squirming baby. Jim Bo followed, carrying a folded play pen in one hand and a diaper bag in the other.

Little Bo cut loose with scream.

"Sorry, y'all. He's a mite hungry," said Kay.

Bea stayed seated on the swing and stretched out her arms. "Don't pass him to anyone else. Jim Bo, fish me a bottle out of that bag. That's a hungry cry if ever I heard one."

David turned to Dotty, "Can you stay for supper, or do we need to take care of business first?"

Dotty glanced at her watch. "I'm sorry. I don't have much time. I'll have to take a rain check on the meal."

"All right, let's get started. I wanted to give everyone an update of what's happened since Kay and Jim Bo arrived." David shifted his gaze to the new parents. "This afternoon the sheriff's department came to your house with a search warrant signed by Judge Rhoades."

Fear flashed across Kay's face at the mention of the sheriff's department and the judge. Jim Bo clenched his fists.

David continued, "They found an opened bottle of vodka

in a kitchen cabinet and two cans of beer in the refrigerator. They also found pills in your medicine cabinet."

Jim Bo shot to his feet. "That does it. That violates my probation for sure, not counting leaving the county without permission."

David held his palms out. "Hold on, Jim Bo. I haven't told you the good news yet. Cameras captured everything. Quint Fowler has an arrest warrant for the lieutenant who planted the pills and booze."

Kay's head bobbed up and down and she mumbled, "Only those with something on their collar are crooked."

"What's that, Kay?" asked CJ.

Kay and Jim Bo exchanged glances. When Jim Bo's baseball cap dipped, Kay continued.

"It's the sheriff and anyone with the rank of lieutenant and above. The sergeants do all the real work of running the jail. They're all okay, as far as I can tell. It's the ranking officers that are crooked. They don't do much, except remind people like me I'd better not get out of line. They find inmates they can make special deals with."

"What kind of deals?" asked CJ.

"If their family has money, inmates can get just about anything they want. A lieutenant will meet the folks at the gate and escort them to the sheriff's office where money is exchanged. Sometime later, usually in the middle of the night, drugs or cigarettes or whatever will be thrown in the inmate's cell. When you see an officer with rank on his collar wearing blue latex gloves, a delivery is being made."

"Thanks, Kay," said David. "That's exactly what I needed. I'll tell Quint who to go after."

Bea stopped feeding Bo for a minute, tilted him up and patted his back. A substantial burp put a grin on everyone's face and lightened the mood. He jerked his head back and opened his mouth for the second half of supper.

CJ looked at David. "Sounds like Biff, doesn't he?"

David smiled and nodded. He continued his part of the briefing. "Tomorrow, a certain lieutenant will be arrested." His gaze turned to Kay and Jim Bo. "But tonight, I need more information. After supper, CJ and I would like to talk with you privately. The more details you give me, the more people will be arrested. One by one, we're going to take away the sheriff's helpers. Then, down he goes."

David sat and Dotty stood. She spoke in quick bursts. "There's more than one way to catch crooks. I'm no longer a spokeswoman for the Highway Patrol so my hands aren't tied like they used to be. Elections are in November. That means the sheriff, Judge Rhoades, the district clerk and the district attorney are all up for re-election. My job will be to make sure the press is at the right place at the right time so they don't miss a newsworthy story. It starts tomorrow when the lieutenant is arrested. Film crews will cover that story and also try to interview the judge and the sheriff. If they choose to speak on camera, they'll have to answer tough questions. If they refuse, they'll appear to be hiding something. Either way, public opinion will begin to shift. Chances are they'll start to blame each other."

"One arrest won't make much difference, will it?" asked Billy Paul.

"From what we now know, I expect there'll be many more arrests of ranking officers in the sheriff's department. That's why it's so important that Kay and Jim Bo tell us everything about the jail."

David took over and slowed the pace as he looked at Kay and then Jim Bo. "In a little over a week, you'll complete your sentence. Judge Rhoades has been notified that you're in the custody of Texas Rangers. That's close enough to the truth. He knows he can't come after you for leaving the county without permission. The video of the lieutenant planting the booze and pills in your home will be released tomorrow after the arrest. The plan to set you up will be exposed. You'll be safe here and there's nothing the judge can do about it."

Jim Bo nodded silently as Kay reached for his hand.

"So far, so good," said Dotty as she continued to look at Kay and Jim Bo. "I'd like for you to do something for me. I made a tentative deal with a Houston television station reporter to come here and interview you. The reporter can ask anything she wants, but her station will only air the various parts of the report as we tell them to."

"Why is that?" asked Billy Paul.

"We want this story to leak out slowly. When dealing with corruption of this type it takes the public a while to get the message. One story is like a drop of water. Story after story keeps adding to it until the glass is full. Then, it overflows."

Billy Paul grumbled, "I don't see how those folks kept getting elected."

Kay answered. "You don't understand. Judge Rhoades, the sheriff, and the district attorney all spend a lot of money doing good things for the community. That's not to mention Charlene Rhoades-Shipley, the County Clerk. Every time you read a newspaper, you'll see one of their smiling faces passing out a check."

"That may be," said David. "But I bet the money came out of someone else's pocket."

CJ saw Kay's knuckles turn white as she gripped the arms of the chair. Her courage needed bolstering. "Bea will be here with you if you need her. Are you willing to do what Dotty wants?"

After exchanging a long glance with Kay, Jim Bo found his voice. "It's the least we can do for all you've done for us. Besides, others are still trapped."

David nodded. "We'll practice tonight. I'll interview you

while CJ videos. The recording will be sent to Quint Fowler so he can fill in the gaps of his investigation."

Dotty broke in. "Tomorrow night I'll come back and act like I'm a television reporter. They ask questions differently from the way David does. We'll tape it and let you see what you look like on camera. By the time the real reporter gets here, you'll be used to being interviewed."

Dotty looked to everyone gathered. "I need to go. I'll be back tomorrow."

CHAPTER TWENTY-THREE

B ea shushed Kay's protest. "I wouldn't have offered if I didn't want to watch little Bo. You folks run off to the barn and take care of all your law enforcement business." She took the smiling baby from his mother's arms and headed toward the back door. "Billy Paul and I will be rolling around on the new carpet with this future fullback."

CJ helped David arrange the chairs and two shop lights. She locked the camera in place on a tripod and stayed behind it in case someone moved out of frame. David turned to Jim Bo and Kay. "Have a seat, and we'll get started."

Following an introduction, David asked Kay and Jim Bo for biographical data.

The first question of substance went to Jim Bo. "What happened when they arrested you?"

"They caught me fair and square. Back then I drank ever' day. I didn't think a thing about driving while pulling down a cold beer. In fact, I had three prior arrests and two convictions. I should've been sent to prison."

"Why didn't they revoke you?" asked David.

"I heard in jail that if I posted a cash bond, I could stay on probation."

"Tell me about that," continued David.

"Bail hadn't been set and I knew I didn't have a chance. A captain came to my cell and asked me if I wanted to stay out of prison. He told me he could arrange it so I'd get probation again if I paid ten thousand dollars cash to the district clerk and didn't go through a bail bondsman. Heck, I had that much saved. I told him it sounded good to me. That's when he said I'd never see the money again. If I ever asked for it, I'd be off to prison. If I'd known I'd meet and marry Kay, and what they'd do to her, I'd never done it."

David turned to Kay. "How did you come to work at the jail?"

The words came out slow and low. "Well...it was after...Jim Bo and I, uh, married—"

Jim Bo interrupted his wife. "Let me backtrack a minute. Kay's nervous and I'm not used to talking with a camera looking at me."

"Take your time, said David. "So you paid the money, then what?"

"I straightened up my life. I quit drinking, met Kay, and we tied the knot. Someone must've found out she'd been a jailer before she moved to Brazoria County. Not long after we married, we got a late-night visit from the same captain that told me how to get probation. He told us Kay needed to apply at the jail or I'd be on my way to prison. He also told her he expected to receive an envelope with three hundred dollars cash in it every payday. She got paid twice a month, so that added up to a fair chunk of her salary."

David looked at Kay, "How long did you pay this?"

Her chin dropped. "I delivered an envelope twice a month for almost six years."

"Were there other employees delivering similar envelopes?"

Kay furrowed her brow. "I can give you names of eight besides me. I believe there's more, but that's not the sort of thing you talk about. I worked the second shift and there's two other shifts."

Kay rattled off the names of the people she'd seen deliver cash-filled envelopes.

"Are there other ways the sheriff or the ranking officers receive kickbacks or bribes?"

"I already told you about how families and friends pay for contraband to come into the jail," said Kay.

"Tell me again. Be specific."

Kay retold the story with more details.

"Any other ways?"

Kay's lip began to quiver. "One other way. It's only happened twice that I'm aware of."

David sensed this would be the most important part of the interview. He lowered his voice. "I realize this is hard, but you need to tell me about it."

After a deep breath, Kay sat up straight. "I hadn't worked at the jail but a couple of months. They called it an escape, but that's not what happened. The chief deputy in charge of the jail, a major, worked late the night this happened. They assigned me to the control picket, and he came and relieved me. A major never stoops to that low a job, but he did that night."

David interrupted, "The control picket officer opens two interior gates, right?"

"At our jail they also operate the front gate. A video camera shows you who wants in. You communicate with them through a speaker. After you let them through double gates, they come into the main building. They go into a second set of double gates with a holding area between them.

It reminds me of a sale barn for cattle auctions with the multiple gates. Only one opens at a time. Thick Plexiglas overlooks the second holding area, the one inside the building. Nobody can get into or out of that area unless the officer in the control picket opens the electric doors."

"Go on."

"The major told me to go to the chow hall and get a cup of coffee. The shift sergeant and the officer in charge of cell block four were drinking coffee and eating cookies when I got there. Twenty minutes later a lieutenant told me to go back to my post. Later that night, when we counted, it didn't clear. They never found the escapee. I heard they didn't search very hard."

David scratched his chin. "Do you believe somebody paid for this to happen?"

Kay looked beyond David. "The story is, a Venezuelan politician big into oil didn't want his son in a Texas prison. An officer I talked to said the inmate bragged about not staying long. I heard it cost his dad a million dollars to get him out. I also heard a plane on Judge Rhoades' private airstrip took him away."

"And the second time?"

Kay touched the jagged scar on her forehead. "Another deal. This time for a half million dollars." She shifted her gaze to David. "The inmate that left this scar and later tried to kill CJ..." Her voice trailed off. She couldn't go on.

Jim Bo took over. "Kay told me the money came from his motorcycle gang. Drug money from selling crystal meth." Jim Bo's jaw tightened. "Your wife took care of him."

Kay struggled as she spoke. "The same routine, but the major wasn't working that night. A captain relieved the shift sergeant and the officer guarding a cell block. A lieutenant took my place in the control picket and told me to take a break. The idiot captain left the key in the lock. Instead of the biker keeping the door to the cell block closed until I passed, he yanked open the door and jumped me." She looked up with pleading eyes. "All he had to do was wait until I passed by. Instead, he took the key in his hand and beat me to a pulp with it. I almost died."

"And the lieutenant?"

"Like I said, in the control picket."

"And the ranking officer in charge of the jail?"

"The captain watched the whole thing. He never lifted a finger to help me."

The story took its toll on Kay, but she continued through her tears. "Someone dragged me to the parking lot. They made it look like that's where the attack took place. At least that's the way one set of reports reads. They said I abandoned my post to go smoke a cigarette. I don't even smoke."

"They didn't fire you for that?"

Kay shook her head. "That's not the way things work. Once they have you, they keep you."

CJ's fingernails dug into the palms of her hands. She relaxed her clenched fists as David continued in an emotionless voice.

"And the other set of reports?"

"It says me and the inmate had a thing going on and I let him escape. The sheriff told me he'd file criminal charges if I didn't keep my mouth shut. That report's in the safe in his office. Now and then he'd make me read it out loud and tell me he could still file charges."

Moths and an array of other summer bugs fluttered in front of and around the bright shop lights. CJ swatted away a pesky winged creature from her face.

"You mentioned a safe in the sheriff's office. Tell me about that," said David.

Kay heaved a sigh, "It's a big safe. I'm not sure what all's in it, other than my report." She stopped and corrected herself. "I did see inside it once when the sheriff showed me the second set of reports. It had stacks of cash."

"The sheriff showed you the report himself?"

Kay nodded. "Every few months."

David motioned to CJ. She rose and turned off the camera with a hand shaking with rage.

CJ marched from the barn to the house. She heard David make a vain attempt at casual conversation, but no one joined him. Even the sight of Billy Paul on the floor with Bo balanced on his belly didn't lighten the mood. The air crackled with pent-up emotion. The four adults and little Bo departed for their separate homes for the night.

Billy Paul's truck had barely cleared the driveway before CJ's pent-up anger shook the house. "We're supposed to forgive, but that story Kay told cuts it. What they did to her and what they did to your family is making my brain boil. Don't say anything else about forgiveness until we see some people behind bars."

David's head bobbed in agreement. "To everything there is a season. It's been a long road, but we're coming to the end of it. Let's make sure we don't blow everything by acting foolish. I tried that and almost lost everything."

CJ threw her hands up and headed for a hot bath. "You're not going to cheat me out of being mad. There's nothing in this world that gets me twisted tighter than cops making victims out of innocent people. If you don't want to hear some words you may not like, go outside."

The better part of an hour passed. CJ wore sleep shorts and a T-shirt when she joined David on the back-porch swing.

"Finished?"

"I guess so," she huffed.

"Feel better?"

"Some." She looked to the river. "I'm still having a hard time balancing justice and forgiveness."

David's gaze joined his wife's. "Me, too."

David's arm looped over her shoulder. She scooted next to him and rested her head on his chest. "My vote is for justice, then forgiveness."

His hand stroked her hair. "Mine too. Let's put some people in jail."

CHAPTER TWENTY-FOUR

"Hi, Mom. Ten more minutes and you would've missed us." CJ rinsed two coffee cups and placed them in the dishwasher. "David's packing the car."

Sandy entered through her doggie door and looked at her with ears down.

"Mom, Sandy's giving me her abandoned child look. What time can I tell her you'll be here?"

CJ listened to the response and spoke to her furry daughter. "Granny Grace and LeRoy will be here about seven this evening."

Ears picked up and a yellow tail beat a strong rhythm. Sandy followed close on CJ's heels as she continued the conversation while walking to the bedroom. "Ever since Jim Bo, Kay and little Bo left, Sandy's been down in the dumps. She follows me everywhere I go.

"What's that, Mom? Yes, they rented a nice little house in the country. It's not far from the rock quarry."

Toothbrushes and toiletries fell into a cloth tote bag. "The pool is finished and so is the landscaping. Be sure to bring your swimsuits. We won't be back until Tuesday afternoon. The television station in Houston wants to do a live interview with David's dad on their evening news. We'll stay in a hotel in Houston the first night he's out of prison and take our time coming home."

David entered the bedroom, came behind her, leaned over, and whispered something meant for her ears only.

"Mom says 'hello' and for you to behave yourself."

"Hello, Grace." His voice sounded anything but repentant.

CJ removed one of David's hands and spun away from the other. All the while she didn't miss a beat in her conversation. "The house is a mess. All the new stuff is still in boxes. Bea and the interior designer will be here first thing tomorrow to help. Emily is the designer's name. She has everything sketched out on a computer program."

After retrieving a handful of hanging clothes, David pointed to a clock on his nightstand.

"I've got to go, Mom. David's so ready to see his dad he may leave without me. Thanks for coming to help. Tell LeRoy hello. Love you, too."

David's phone chimed an incoming call before CJ's seat-belt clicked. "Quint. What's wrong?"

"David, is CJ with you?"

"She's right here."

"Go ahead, Quint," said CJ.

"You're driving into a hornet's nest. We arrested another lieutenant at the sheriff's office. That makes three and one captain. The sheriff knows we're closing the net on him and Dotty has the press acting like bloodhounds. Judge Rhoades is quiet in public but he's burning up the phones to local and state politicians."

David interrupted. "We expected that. Is there something new with Dad?"

"That's why I called. Judge Rhoades signed a bench

warrant an hour ago. It instructs the sheriff to pick up your dad and bring him to the county jail on Sunday afternoon."

David's grip on the steering wheel tightened and his brow took on the appearance of a washboard. "Quint, we can't let that happen. He'll never make it to court alive."

"Hold on. It's taken care of. I called the prison's regional director. He's arranged for your dad to be transferred."

Concern morphed into near panic in David's voice. "Where are they taking him?"

Quint allowed himself a conspirator's laugh. "That depends on who you ask. There are over fifty prison units in the state. As we speak, the records department in Huntsville is making a bunch of mistakes with your dad's paperwork. If anyone asks, they'll show your dad being transferred to a dozen different places. Officially your dad will be in transit. He'll stay that way until he arrives at the hearing."

CJ broke in. "Where will he really be?"

"That's the best part." Quint couldn't contain a laugh.

David spoke through clenched teeth. "Quint, this may be fun for you, but I'm in no mood for it."

"You'll like this. It's Friday morning now. Early tomorrow, I'm picking up a bench warrant from the judge that supervises Judge Rhoades. Your dad will be long-gone by the time the sheriff tries to pick him up on Sunday."

"Where are you taking him?" asked CJ.

"Fishing. We'll be at Biff's bay house from tomorrow evening until I take him to court."

Her shoulders relaxed. "If I wasn't a happily married woman, I'd give you a big kiss."

David slumped in his seat. "Thanks, Quint." He paused a second and furrowed his brow again. "I'm still concerned about Dad after he goes to court. What if the judge or the sheriff try something else?"

"I have a little surprise for the judge if he does. The

sheriff is a different story. There's something about your dad that has him scared."

CJ interjected, "Quint, I have something rattling around in my mind. David and I will talk it over and discuss it with you tonight."

"Sounds good. Are we still on for six-thirty?"

"Six-thirty in the lobby. We'll decide where to go from there," said David.

CHAPTER TWENTY-FIVE

A sign on a tripod stand in the hotel lobby welcomed the alumni of David's class. He obtained plastic card-keys for their reserved room and pushed a cart loaded with their bags and hanging clothes toward the elevator.

The hotel room didn't disappoint. It boasted the extravagance of a jetted tub, chocolates on the pillows and a separate living area apart from the bedroom.

CJ sat upright when David's phone broke the calm of the room.

Her husband's face contorted. His voice came out tight and tinny. Quick single syllable responses were followed by, "I'll get there as soon as I can."

CJ tried to speak, but David held up a hand to stop her. His eyes darted back and forth. It didn't take long before his words poured out as if a dam had been breached. "The sheriff came two days early. The warden's stalling. I have to get Dad. Quint's on his way to get the bench warrant. He'll fax it to the warden as soon as he can."

David paced. "We need another vehicle." He spun toward

the door. "Make sure it's something inconspicuous, and rent it under your maiden name. Text me when you have it."

The door closed behind him with a resounding thud.

———

THE THIRTY-FIVE-MILE DRIVE took David forty-five minutes due to traffic. He weaved around the cars he could and cursed the slow pace. Turning off a main highway, he sped up on a narrow blacktop road. Buildings constructed of red, prison-made bricks loomed in the distance. He approached the prison's parking lot and waited as the sheriff's car backed out of a parking space reserved for law enforcement. It drove to a narrow blacktop road that encircled the prison. David knew from experience only two gates existed in Texas prisons: one in the front for foot-traffic and a sally-port in the back large enough to handle cars, trucks and buses.

He wheeled his state-issued SUV into the vacated reserved parking space and made for the front gate.

Warden McCade met him at the building's entrance with a firm handshake. "Glad you made it. The sheriff's fit to be tied. I told him he couldn't take a prisoner out the front gate."

"I saw him driving around the perimeter. What's up?"

"I sent him to the back gate. He'll really be mad when he finds out your father is no longer here. I'll let him wait long enough for you to be long gone."

"Will you have to tell him I took him?"

A sly smile came across the warden's face. "If he presses me, I'll apologize for not knowing he left earlier today. Officially, your dad's in transit. The sheriff will need to call the Bureau of Classifications and Records in Huntsville to find out exactly where."

"What will they say?"

"It depends on who he talks to. If he calls three times, he'll get three different answers."

David nodded. The flow of stomach acid tapered off. "In other words, we're back to our original plan."

"Original plan, only a day early." The warden opened the door to his secretary's office. "Here he is, all dressed out in street clothes and ready to go."

David's heart skipped a beat when his father lunged into his arms and wouldn't let go. After the extended bear hug, father and son separated. "Dad, I hate to do this, but we need to make this look official." David reached behind his back and pulled out chrome handcuffs. As a concession, he fastened his father's hands in front instead of behind his back.

"Keep the key handy, son. I'm ready to start acting like a free man."

Quick but heartfelt thanks from both men brought a smile to the warden's face. Was it satisfaction in seeing justice served, amusement from deceiving a crooked sheriff, or being relieved of a job-threatening inmate? It didn't matter. The man had done his job and David had his father.

With long strides the unlikely father and son duo walked to the front gate. The metallic click of freedom sounded as the gates opened and then slammed shut. "Dad, let's put you in the back seat. I saw two deputies waiting up the road. They're insurance for the sheriff. Lay down when I tell you to."

Maintaining an even speed, they left prison property. Robert dipped below the windows and David casually lifted a hand to wave at the two deputies in their cars. He reached for his handcuff key and passed it to his father's outstretched manacled hands. "If you can't get those off, I'll pull over."

"Keep driving, son. Don't stop for anything. By the way, where are we going?"

"Listen to the phone calls. That'll tell you what's going on."

David punched a name on his phone and put it on speaker. "I have him, Quint. We're heading to the hotel. I'll have CJ rent a room for Dad under her maiden name. I'll text the room number to you. We'll take care of all the other plans tonight."

Robert ignored the seatbelt law and stuck his head forward. "Why didn't you bring your wife? I can't wait to meet her."

"She's taking care of errands."

"Shouldn't you call her?"

"I will. Let me get my heart out of my throat."

Five miles passed. Another call interrupted their father-son conversation.

"Do you have him? Is everything all right? Where are you?" demanded CJ.

"Slow down Catherine. We're away from the prison and headed to the hotel. Where are you?"

The pitch of her voice rose. "Why didn't you call me? I've been worried sick."

Robert spoke in an omniscient tone. "I told you to call her."

"I heard that," said CJ. "You need to pay attention to your father."

David bristled. Some things didn't change with time. With two against one he couldn't win. Time to change the subject. "Where are you?"

"I'm leaving the rental car agency. I had to call Uber to get here. How does a dark blue mini-van with dark windows sound?"

"Perfect. I have another job for you. As soon as you get to the hotel, rent another room for dad. Make sure you put it under your maiden name and try to get it as close to our room as possible."

"Anything else?" asked CJ.

"Call me back as soon as you get the room."

"I'll send you a text. What's your ETA?"

"Twenty-five minutes."

"Are you sure you don't want him in our room?"

"We're going to carry on like he isn't here. It will be safer for him."

Silent seconds passed. "I don't like it," said CJ. "He needs a way of contacting us if someone tries to get in his room. Something besides the hotel phone."

David considered her objection. "After you get a room, go buy a burner phone. Program our numbers into it." He glanced in the rear-view mirror. "While you're shopping, get dad some new clothes that don't look prison made. He's my build, only two inches shorter."

"Size twelve cross-trainers," shouted Bob from the back seat.

"Consider it done. I'll be gone when you get here. His door will be rigged so you can get in."

A click ended the call. When CJ had a mission to accomplish, she exercised an economy of words.

Robert said, "Wow. That's one smart woman you married."

David looked in the rear-view mirror. "I'd say she's brilliant. She has to be to keep up with me."

A huff came from the back seat. "You weren't too brilliant the time I had to rebuild the carburetor on your first car."

"That's Biff's fault. He said he could get me ten more miles per gallon with a simple adjustment."

"And you believed that knuckle head? I rest my case."

David and his father burst into laughter at the same time. How good to hear his father's laugh, like an old sweater you

151

pulled out on a cold morning. Like old times? No. That could never be.

Anger ignited afresh. This forgiveness thing. How? Once again an image of his mother flashed before his eyes.

His father's hand rested on his shoulder. "I miss her too."

Miles passed in comfortable silence until David's phone jangled a text notification. It read *439*.

The SUV eased into a parking spot near a side door to the hotel. David scanned the area. His father narrowly missed an attempt on his life in prison and they averted another major threat less than an hour ago. People wanted his dad dead. He had to keep him safe.

CHAPTER TWENTY-SIX

A green light flashed and a metallic click sounded as David slid his key card into a reader on the side entrance to the hotel. The two men bounded up four flights of stairs. David opened the fire door, but only enough to get a glimpse of an empty hallway. Voices burst into the hall as a door to a room opened. He eased the door shut and drew his pistol. The chrome-plated .45 slid back in its holster as the women's voices faded. "Let's go, Dad." A mere nudge opened the door to room 439.

David removed a wad of tissue and tape from the latch on the door, scanned the room, checked the bathroom, and even flung back the door to a small closet. A note lay on the bed. David read it before he realized CJ had addressed it to his father.

Welcome! What do you want me to call you? I'm partial to Dad, but that might be too informal for your liking. I tried to get you a suite, but couldn't. I'll be back soon. CJ. Or, Catherine Jo, or Catherine—whatever you prefer.

Robert Quisenheimer read the note and looked at his son. "My first name has been *Inmate* for so long, this is going to take some getting used to."

"I hope the room is all right," said David in an echo of his wife's sentiments.

His father seemed to drink in the luxury of the room with his eyes. His gaze lingered on the flat-screen television, mini-refrigerator, microwave and lacquered desk. He paused and examined a card. "Do all hotels offer internet connections?"

"It's standard these days," said David with a lump in his throat.

"I'd like to get a lap-top."

"There's a brand new one waiting for you at home. I should have brought it."

"You didn't have to do that."

"I'm behind on birthday and Christmas presents."

David chewed on his bottom lip. How much life had his father been cheated out of?

Bob moved to the king-sized bed and caressed a down duvet. He shuffled to the bathroom's door and looked in. "I've not showered by myself in sixteen years. The first thing I'm going to do is wash off the smell of prison." He stepped into the bathroom. "I'd forgotten how good a fluffy towel could feel. When did they start putting lavender lotion in hotel rooms?" Seeing David's worried face, he said, "I'll be fine. You and CJ go on. Pretend I'm not here."

David stepped to the door. "Make sure you don't open this for anyone but me or CJ. If you're hungry, I can call room service. I'll have it delivered to my room and bring it to you."

His father's gaze darted from one unfamiliar item to the next. "This may sound strange, but I need some time by myself. It's going to take me a while to get used to a place where they don't count you every few hours."

As David reached for the door knob, his dad's voice stopped him. "I want to visit your mother's grave in the morning."

David took a deep breath. "That might not be a good idea."

"Good or not, I'm going. I've waited too long to say goodbye."

A lump the size of a golf ball stuck in David's throat. "All right, Dad. We'll do it."

His father turned to the mirror and examined the aged face looking back at him. His hands reached out to the marble sink-top to keep him from falling.

The long years in a steel and concrete box had taken their toll. Prisons aren't much on amenities. Bright lights over a mirror the size of a sheet of plywood showed the ravages of time and confinement. In prison, inmates aren't permitted anything but a hand-held mirror they buy from the prison commissary. David held the man who'd done nothing but love him all his life. The mirror caught the reflection of four streams of tears.

Minutes passed. David didn't release his father until he felt him straighten his spine and throw back his shoulders.

"Go. Don't come back for at least three hours."

David sensed his father needed to climb out of a deep well of regret. "I'll give the secret knock when I come back."

The wry smile David had not seen in years returned to his father's face. "Shave-and-a-haircut isn't much of a secret knock. Perhaps we should come up with something new."

"No way. It worked for the first sixteen years of my life; it's good enough for the rest of it."

The door closed behind David and he heard the extra latch click into the metal door frame. The irony of the moment struck him. Father and son wanted nothing more than to spend time together, but they couldn't. Not yet. He likened it to going from a dark room into brilliant sunlight. Too much, too fast. It hurt in its own way. Adjustment would take time.

With hours to kill, he decided to check out the ballroom where the reunion would be held.

CHAPTER TWENTY-SEVEN

Two women with familiar faces placed letter jackets, yearbooks, photos, and vintage CD's on tables outside the double doors to the ballroom. They looked up from their jabbering. The first placed her hand over her mouth as the second shrieked. In unison they exclaimed, "David! Oh my God, it's David." Two sets of arms opened wide as they possibly could and streaked toward him.

David fell victim to their embraces. It came as a shock how much he appreciated their heart-felt acceptance.

"Hi, Lucy. Arlene? Is that you?"

"I knew you'd be here," exclaimed Lucy, the shorter of the two. "As soon as I heard they overturned your father's conviction, I called Arlene. I said, 'Arlene, David Quisenheimer will be at this year's reunion.' And here you are."

Before David could speak, Arlene took over. "Lucy, you stop right there. I called you. I was putting the story together for print and called you the minute I finished."

Claim and counter-claims filled the air. With fingers pointing at each other they caught themselves in mid-squabble, grabbed each other's index finger, and broke into a riotous laugh.

"Anyway," declared Lucy, "it's wonderful to see you. We've prayed for you for years."

Arlene took over. "We didn't have a choice. Biff wouldn't let us forget. That man got religion eight years ago and put you and your dad on every prayer list he could find. How did that practical joker turn out to be such a nice guy?"

"WOOO...PIG...SOOIE!" The sound came from within the ballroom. Smiles spread across all three faces as Biff approached.

"Hello, ladies and germ," said Biff.

"Biff," exclaimed Arlene. "It's David Quisenheimer."

Biff screwed up his face. "David? I don't know anyone named David." He wrapped both arms around his buddy, lifted him up and turned a circle. "Where's that wife of yours? I need to get back at her for that dirty trick she pulled on me."

"Do it at your own risk. She had to run some errands but she'll be back any minute."

Biff released his grip. "I'll find her."

Left alone with Lucy and Arlene, David fielded questions until another familiar figure approached. This one stood about five-feet-nine-inches tall and weighed in the neighborhood of two hundred and ten pounds. His blond hair parted not far above his left ear. With the aid of styling gel and hair spray, the locks reached over an obviously bald dome and stuck to the ring of hair on the opposite side.

"Well, well, if it isn't David Quisenheimer."

The slimy way the words oozed out caused David to bristle.

Before he could respond, Arlene stepped toe-to-toe and nose-to-nose with the intruder. "Stephen Shipley, don't you dare start. Everyone knows David's dad is being released because he's innocent. If your bread wasn't buttered on both sides by that crooked judge and the idiot DA, you might be able to recognize the truth."

"That's right, Shipwreck," added Lucy as she took two steps forward and tented her hands on her hips. "If that creep you work for had been interested in doing what's right, David's dad would have been released a long time ago. I can't wait until the next election. There's going to be a house-cleaning in this county that's going to curl what little hair you have left."

Shipwreck Shipley backed up and held out his palms. "Hold on, you two. I had nothing to do with the delays. Besides, you don't understand how the system works. Once a person is found guilty, it's the duty of the district attorney to protect the sanctity of the jury's decision."

Both women took another step forward. The assistant district attorney took two steps back.

Arlene's eyes narrowed. "Stuff a sock in it, Shipwreck. Nobody's buying what you're selling any more."

Sidestepping the trio, Shipley headed for the lobby. Lucy fired a final verbal shot as he slunk away. "It might be a good idea if you and your wife and her daddy started looking for other jobs."

David gave each woman a heartfelt hug. "Thanks. I didn't know how our classmates would react."

Lucy, face still red, smoothed the front of her blouse. "Every time I turn on the news or read the paper there's a new story about corruption. Everyone is sick to death of seeing the sheriff's face and watching Judge Rhoades duck and dodge questions."

Arlene added, "And that DA is as slick as a bag of worms with runny noses."

"Charlie isn't much better," huffed Lucy.

Arlene thrust out her chin. "That's Charlene to us peasants, thank you very much."

Lucy hooked her arm in Arlene's and looked at David. "I didn't plan to start until later, but that impersonator of an assistant district attorney has driven me to drink. Why don't we three go to the bar and take some shipwreck medicine?"

David smiled. "You two go ahead. I'll take a look at the decorations." He chuckled as the women walked to the lobby. Lucy and Arlene's defense of him proved Shipwreck Shipley fought against a raging sea of public opinion.

How hard do people fight to keep from drowning?

CHAPTER TWENTY-EIGHT

Hands grabbed CJ below the ribs as she strode across the Hotel's lobby. Her squeal caused the desk clerk's head to snap upward as the contents of her sacks scattered over the marble floor.

"Got-cha!" said a familiar voice.

"Biff Stewart! I should have known," huffed CJ.

"Hello, Wonder Woman. I understand there's a fishing trip planned for this weekend, and it includes a special guest."

CJ bent down to pick up the contents of white plastic bags. "Shhh. Nobody's supposed to know. David wants me to go. Can Amy come?"

Biff kneeled and began to stuff items into one of the bags. "There's no way my parents will keep the kids more than one night. The last time we left them two nights they almost cost me my inheritance."

"Do I want to hear this?"

"They super-glued the lid and seat to the porcelain commode in my parent's master bathroom. Dad didn't come close to making it to the hall bath. Talk about mad!"

CJ bit her tongue and cast her gaze past him. To allow Biff

to gain eye contact would result in laughter and laughter encouraged him.

"Are you and Amy staying here tomorrow night?" she asked.

A lecherous smile crept across Biff's face. "I saw a doctor a month and a half ago. We decided to take the guesswork out of there being any more surprises. You might say I have high hopes for tomorrow night."

CJ groaned.

Biff careened on. "At least being here will ensure some privacy. Our third child likes to play with the camera on his cell phone. Pictures and film go on Facebook. Amy made me put three locks on our bedroom door after he posted a special Christmas greeting."

She shook her head. "I never know if you're telling the truth or making everything up. How do you do that?"

"Speaking of stories, I have one for you." He grimaced and placed a hand over his stomach. "No time for the story now. You wouldn't happen to have a Sports Illustrated in your purse, would you?"

"No. Why?"

"I switched cereal bowls with my oldest boy this morning. His little sister likes to put laxative in his Frosted Flakes. I need to run before I wind up like my dad."

"Enough!" said CJ. "No more potty jokes." Biff only laughed. She couldn't help but smile at his goofy grin. "Have you seen David?"

"He's in the ballroom. At least that's where I left him a few minutes ago." Biff rubbed his belly. "I hate to rush, but some things can't be put off."

In his haste Biff narrowly missed running into a planter box on his way to the men's room.

DAVID CONCLUDED his tour of the ballroom, passed Biff as he scurried by, and walked to the lobby in search of his wife. He crept up on her blind side and spoke in a husky voice. "Hello, doll. Have we met or have you only been in my dreams?"

CJ turned and played along. "I don't believe I've had the pleasure, but we might be able to do something about that. What did you have in mind?"

"I don't have anything to do for the next couple of hours. We could think of something."

CJ drew a hand down his chest. "If you have a room, I could come up for a while."

A movement on the other side of the planter box caught David's eye. Looking past his wife he saw Shipwreck Shipley pushing aside a palm branch. From where he stood, all Shipwreck could see was CJ's back.

"We have an enemy spy watching us," whispered David. "Make it look like I'm trying to pick you up."

"That's not what you were doing?"

David pointed to the bags she held in front of her. With ample volume for Shipley to hear, he said, "I'll need to see the merchandise. I want to make sure I get my money's worth."

CJ held a plastic sack in front of her. The burn phone lay on top of an assortment of snacks and clothes. As David cast his gaze into the bag she said, "You look like a man that likes quality."

"Not bad. How much?"

"Three hundred bucks for everything."

"That seems fair. Let's go upstairs and examine what you've got in more detail."

It took all the willpower David could muster to wait until they were on the elevator before erupting in laughter.

BIFF SAT in the fourth stall of the bathroom, catching up on Facebook posts. A voice bounced off the porcelain tiles.

"Sheriff. This is Stephen Shipley. I have something big. I'm at the new hotel in Lake Jackson. We're setting up for our class reunion. Guess who's here."

"Ok, you don't have time for games. It's David Quisenheimer. That's right, the son of Robert Quisenheimer. Anyway, I overheard him proposition a hooker in the lobby. He's taking her to his room right now."

"Yes, I'm sure. They agreed on a price, three hundred dollars." Shipley's voice stopped. "No, I don't know what room. Do you want me to find out?"

Biff bit down on his bottom lip.

"I'll wait for you in the lobby...What do you mean, you don't have time?" Shipwreck lowered his voice. "All right, quit yelling. A lieutenant and some deputies will have to do."

The bathroom door bounced shut. Biff strode to the sink to wash his hands. He looked up, smiled and nodded at his reflection. "This is it. I'll hang this over CJ's head the rest of her life. I need to find Arlene. Wait, I'd better call Quint Fowler first."

Lucy and Arlene sat on stools in the bar nursing glasses of pink wine. Biff approached with a question. "Arlene, how would you like to get a story that'll make national news?"

Arlene's right hand looked like a flipper on a pinball machine. She dismissed the practical jokester with, "Trying to pull another fast one? It won't work."

"This is no joke. Sheriff's deputies are on their way to this hotel. They're going to arrest a cop who's a special assistant to the Texas Rangers. They think he's in his room with a prostitute, but she's his wife."

"Ha, that story won't make national news."

Biff held up both palms as stop signs. "Let me finish. The cop is David. You probably don't know it, but he changed his name to David Harper before we graduated. He's been a decorated soldier, a highway patrolman and now he works with the Rangers. His wife's maiden name is CJ David. She's the assistant chief of police at Agape Christian University."

A light of recognition came into Arlene's eyes. "Is that the same CJ David who killed the biker that escaped from our county jail? Wasn't she selected to be a Texas Ranger?"

Biff nodded. "That's her."

Arlene and Lucy slid off their barstools. Biff added a final bit of information. "Here's the best part. Shipwreck called the sheriff. I overheard everything he said."

The three stepped quickly toward the lobby, but Arlene gave a final warning. "If you're making this up, Biff Stewart, I'll remind Amy you bought her a toaster for her birthday."

Biff swallowed hard.

"Holy smoke," interrupted Lucy. "Three police cars are rolling up. Here they come. Quick, hide behind the planter until we find out the room they're going to."

Arlene took over in barely audible whispers. "I'll put on my press pass as soon as we get to their floor. You two stay behind me. You each have phones that record video, don't you?" Both nodded. "Good, it's important we all get good recordings. Try not to shake and film as long as you can. If they're arrested, make sure you get a shot of David and his wife in handcuffs. No matter what the deputies say, keep filming."

Lucy looked toward the desk and strained to hear. "There they go. I heard the clerk say four-something."

"That's all we need," said Biff. "Let's wait until the deputies and Shipwreck get in the elevator. We'll take the next one up."

CHAPTER TWENTY-NINE

The elevator door eased open, revealing a long corridor branching out in both directions. Biff, Lucy, and Arlene stepped out with cell phones cupped in their hands. Four uniformed men approached room 417 with hands on pistols. Shipwreck stood behind the policemen and motioned with his hand for the trio of classmates to stay where they were. Lucy, the shortest of the three, stood between Biff and Arlene. She raised her phone and began to film.

"Room service," the voice of the lieutenant followed a crisp knock. The door opened and the quartet of deputies stormed into the room.

Arlene sprinted to the open door with her press pass dangling from a lanyard around her neck. She spoke before they reached the open portal. "Lucy, take low. Biff, take high, I'll take the middle. Cameras only in the doorway." Arlene thrust her cell phone past the door frame and began to film. Biff followed suit. Lucy completed a vertical line of three hands and cell phone cameras pointed into the room.

"Lay across the bed," shouted a deep voice.

"Watch out, there's a weapon on the dresser," said a second voice.

"Sure, there's a gun. I'm a cop."

"Shut up. Put your hands behind your back."

The sound of handcuffs ratcheting drifted into the hallway. Biff bit his index finger in an attempt not to laugh as he peeked around the corner.

"Where's the hooker?" demanded the lieutenant.

One of the officers pounded on the bathroom door. "You! Unlock the door and back away with your hands up." The sound of a lock clicking preceded, "Get out here, hands on the wall. Pat her down, Chuck."

"Nothing on her."

The second deputy spoke, "I found another gun."

CJ's voice sounded as if it came through clenched teeth. "If you idiots would take a minute, you'd find our badges and IDs."

The lieutenant shot back, "Shut up. You can tell your story to a judge."

Deputy Chuck spoke. "Eh, Lieutenant. There's a badge and an ID in the purse. It says she's the Assistant Chief of Police at Agape Christian University."

"Yeah," said the second deputy. "And this guy's ID says he's Sergeant David Harper, with the Department of Public Safety. The badge and ID sure look real."

Stephen Shipley stood in the hallway peering past the trio taking video. "He's no state cop, and that's not his name. It's David Quisenheimer. His dad is the convict that killed his wife. There's no telling what he's up to."

"Get 'em out of here," shouted the lieutenant.

A shove from a tall man sent Shipwreck stumbling down the hall. The man issuing the shove wore a straw Stetson and a narrow-eyed scowl. Brushing past the three doing the filming, he stepped into the room. His gaze shifted from face to face

as he took in the countenance of the lieutenant and his officers. "Will someone tell me why you have a special assistant to
the Rangers and an assistant chief of police in handcuffs?"

"Ranger Fowler," said Shipwreck as he pushed his way into
the room. "I know this man. His name is David Quisenheimer. He offered money to this woman for sex."

Quint Fowler kept his gaze on the lieutenant and raised
his voice. "You, sir, have dug yourself quite a hole. This is
Sergeant Harper and his wife."

"His wife?"

Quint took two steps forward and allowed his gaze to
bore into the lieutenant.

"Did you take the time to check IDs? Wasn't it unusual
for a so-called hooker to have a badge? What about the front
desk? Did you check to see how they registered?"

The lieutenant returned his gaze with a blank stare.

"I'll ask again. Did any of you look at IDs?"

"Yes, sir, we told the lieutenant everything looked real to
us," said Deputy Chuck.

Quint's gaze shifted back and forth from the lieutenant to
his deputies. "The last time I checked the penal code, it's not
against the law for a State Police Officer or an Assistant Chief
of Police to carry a gun. Also, it may surprise you to learn
husbands and wives can rent hotel rooms together." His voice
climbed a ladder of anger. "What is not legal is false arrest
and abuse of office."

The hand of the ranger found the butt of the pearl-
handled pistol on his hip. "If I don't see some handcuffs come
off, and I mean right now, I'll have more state troopers here
than you knew existed." He paused. "And while you're at it,
apologies are in order."

The two deputies fumbled to remove the handcuffs,
saying they were sorry in as many ways as they could come up

with. Shipwreck spun and exited past the filming cell phones. Biff turned and continued to film his classmate until Stephen disappeared into the elevator.

Arlene's words came with speed and authority as she tapped Lucy and Biff, their cue to stop filming. "Lucy, go past the elevator and catch the lieutenant and the deputies as they leave the room. Biff, keep filming David and CJ. I'll go downstairs and get footage of the cops leaving the hotel and driving away. We'll meet in the bar."

Biff made room for Deputy Chuck and another deputy to exit. They shuffled sheepishly into the hallway and mumbled their way to the elevator. He turned to see CJ step between the lieutenant and the doorway. "I hope you enjoyed your career in law enforcement." Her next words could chill the sun. "It's over."

David stood beside CJ. "Give the sheriff a message from me. Tell him I hope he likes prison food. I'm going to do everything I can to put him in the same cell my father had to live in."

Quint Fowler interrupted before David could say anything more. "Lieutenant, it's time for you to leave. Tonight's news will be interesting. You can explain to the sheriff how you became a celebrity."

The room emptied and Biff slipped his phone into his pocket. Quint began to chuckle and David followed suit. Biff looked at CJ and crowed, "Checkmate."

CJ's face, already red with anger, darkened even more. "What's so funny? It's a good thing I didn't have my purse in the bathroom. Somebody would've gone out of here feet first."

The three men's laughter morphed into hysterics. Quint managed to squeak out, "You two...handcuffed...and those three at the door filming."

"What three?" demanded CJ. "I had my head pushed against the wall. I didn't see anything."

David managed to contain his guffaws. "Biff and two of my classmates. One of them works for the newspaper. All three had their cell phones stuck in the doorway. They filmed the whole thing."

Quint added, "I guarantee you'll make Houston news tonight. Wait until Dotty finds out. She'll be ecstatic. This fits her plan perfectly."

CJ plopped onto the couch and hid her face in her hands. Her head wagged back and forth as she moaned, "Biff Stewart, you're behind this and I'll never hear the end of it."

Quint, David, and Biff found new fodder for their laughter, at CJ's expense.

In due time they composed themselves. "I guess this room is as good a place as any," said David as he retrieved a yellow note pad. "Biff, Dad's safe and sound down the hall."

"Down the hall? Now? When did he get out?"

"I'll give you the story later," said David.

CJ looked at Quint. "Bring us up to speed."

Quint parked his lanky frame on a fabric-covered recliner. "Amy managed to rig a tiny camera in the ceiling of the district clerk's office. We have three weeks of video showing Charlene cutting out obituaries every Friday. We also have some good shots of her writing checks and placing entries in the log she keeps locked in her desk."

"That's plenty for a warrant," said David.

"I already have it. Monday morning Mrs. Charlene Rhoades Shipley will be arrested and her log book and computer seized."

"Ah-ha, that's the surprise for the judge you spoke of," said David. "The arrest of his little girl should get the judge's mind off my father."

Quint nodded. "He'll be handed a note before your dad's proceedings. That's just one surprise for him."

CJ's eyes widened. "What else?"

Quint stuck his boots straight out and leaned back. "Let's just say the IRS is interested in knowing how a state district judge who makes about a hundred and seventy thousand dollars a year in total income from salary and investments can afford a castle for a home and an airplane capable of flying non-stop to Central America. Those two are valued at over thirty million dollars. He'll receive a phone call and a certified letter Monday morning informing him of an audit."

"Just like Al Capone," said David.

"What do you mean?" asked Biff.

"Al Capone, the 1930s Chicago gangster," said Quint. "He ran a crime syndicate and nobody would dare testify against him. They nailed him for income tax evasion. He received a seven-year sentence."

"Ah," said CJ. "I remember. By the time the prison door swung open everything had changed. He no longer had an organization that wanted or needed him."

Quint folded up his legs and leaned forward. "All the corruption in this county is related to money. Everyone involved is counting on the cash continuing to flow. The arrests of the county clerk and the sheriff will choke off their money supply. Any funds the judge has will be diverted to pay for tax attorneys and lawyers to represent him. We've checked his bank accounts. There's a lot of money there, but that's not where most of it is hidden. We were able to get a deposition from one of the lieutenants we arrested. The sheriff's safe is where a pile of cash is held. Still, we think there's more somewhere else. The judge will eventually lose his home, expensive toys and he'll see his daughter go to prison."

"It's not enough for all he's done," said CJ.

Quint added, "There's more. The Judicial Review Board is

coming after him for suppressing evidence in the trial of David's dad. They'll also consider the suspicious nature of his daughter misappropriating funds that were linked to his court when he set bail. Finally, it won't look good for him after the IRS audit shows he can't account for his lavish lifestyle. It may take time, but they'll eventually take his license to practice law. It isn't a murder charge, but it's something else that'll drain him financially."

CJ shook her head in disgust. "Are you saying he'll only serve time for some sort of tax evasion charge and possibly as an accessory in the charges related to stealing the bail money?"

"Unless we can get either his daughter or the sheriff to testify against him, or we find something else."

David abruptly changed the subject. "I made a promise to Dad. I need your help tomorrow morning."

"I'm not going to like this, am I?"

"It's a slight detour on your way to the bay house. I have it all planned out."

CHAPTER THIRTY

Dawn broke on a near-perfect September morning. CJ placed a spotter's scope in the seat beside her after scanning the parking lot one more time. Wearing blue jeans, a short-sleeve shirt, and a baseball cap, David exited a side door to the hotel and made for the dark blue mini-van. He walked fast, his head on a swivel. The door to the van clicked shut. "See anything?" he asked.

"Nothing."

"Let's go. We'll ride around for a while."

Quick turns, rapid acceleration and sudden stops in the parking lots of two isolated businesses brought a sigh of relief from David. "No one's following yet. I need to make sure they're not on to us."

David scanned the rear view mirror every three seconds while rocking back and forth. This wasn't like him. She needed to get his mind on something else. "There weren't many people at last night's mixer."

"Huh?"

CJ cast a gaze his way. "Snap out of it. Nothing's going to

happen, and if it does, we'll handle it. Give your mind a rest and tell me why so few people showed up last night."

After one final glance in the rear-view mirror, David leaned back in the seat. "It didn't surprise me. Biff said a lot of people are coming in from out of town. Almost everyone our age has kids. I guess it's hard for them to get away two nights in a row. The big blow-out is tonight. The word is they found a good band that plays the old stuff."

CJ chuckled. "You make it sound like you've been out of high school fifty years instead of fifteen." She started to say something, but held her tongue.

"What? What were you going to say?"

"It wasn't very nice." CJ chose her words with care and proceeded. "Did you see how Mrs. Charlene Rhoades-Shipley acted last night? By the way, what did you ever see in her?"

David glanced out the passenger side window. "That's not the same girl I dated in high school. The Charlie I knew laughed, had fun, and would be the first to join Biff in a practical joke." He glanced her way and grinned. "She also had a great figure and straight blond hair down to her waist."

CJ turned her head and stared at David. How odd to hear her husband, a man she'd known for such a long time, talk about a high school sweetheart with such admiration. A realization struck her. "You were in love with her."

His hand grabbed the steering wheel and steered the van to the left. "Keep it between the ditches, please."

A surge of jealousy flooded into CJ. Last night she talked to a woman her husband had been seriously involved with. Was Charlene to have been Mrs. David Quisenheimer? How many children would they have had by now?

Jealousy gave way to anger. Charlene had a pretty face, but she hadn't aged well. Body and soul needed an overhaul. CJ's voice took on a defensive tone, even though she tried to mask it. "I couldn't believe the way she spoke to Amy."

"You heard that, too?"

"How could I help it? Whatever she drank sure loosened her tongue. How many times did she come to Amy and say the same thing? 'Mrs. Stewart, if you value your job you won't be dancing tomorrow night.' What did she mean?"

David's shoulders rose and fell. "Beats me, but something tells me we may see a side of Amy tonight that'll surprise us."

"Hmmm."

"What does that mean?" asked David.

"Nothing," she snapped.

"Now I know it means something. Whatever it is, you need to tell me."

The words flew from her mouth before she could stop them. "Were you and Charlene planning to get married?"

David's look brought on a third emotion—regret. Her brain froze. And her tongue with it. Words of apology refused to come.

"We lived in a fantasy land of going to the beach and being popular at school." David cast his gaze in her direction. "I never asked her to marry me. I didn't need to. Everyone knew that's what would happen." He paused. His next words came out like course-grit sandpaper. "Her father saw we were getting too serious and put an end to it. I didn't have long to grieve over a teen romance. Mom's murder and dad's arrest happened a week later."

Silence filled the van, the kind of uncomfortable silence words had a hard time breaking through. Miles passed.

CJ reached her hand out. David took it in his, brought it to his lips, kissed it, and said, "That was then, this is now. Let's get our heads straight. Dad's life may depend on it."

A rock fence encircled the cemetery. City streets bracketed all sides. CJ drove a lap around the perimeter and added a second for good measure. Satisfied, she pulled through the main entrance. David said, "I'll point out Mom's gravesite. We'll park away from it."

The van eased to a stop. "Let's go over the plan again," said David in a military cadence. "I want you to walk through the cemetery. Act like you're reading headstones and doing research. I'll take the binoculars and find a place where I have a view of the perimeter and everyone that comes and goes. Dad and Quint will be here by eight-thirty. Quint will drop Dad off and find a place to hide and watch. Be at Mom's grave when Dad gets out. I'll join you as soon as I'm sure no one has followed."

CJ glanced at her watch. They'd allowed plenty of time to search for any of the sheriff's underlings. She crisscrossed a field studded with headstones under oaks dripping with Spanish moss. Each marker bore silent witness to a life lived. Even the most elaborate gave but scant information about the person it guarded. The brevity of earthly life appeared all around her, chiseled in stone. Prayer came easily.

Smack. CJ pulled her hand from her neck and found a nickel-sized smear of blood on it. "Mosquitoes. I hate mosquitoes. I'm wearing a Kevlar vest, I have a nine-millimeter in my waistband and a thirty-eight strapped to my ankle. I still can't protect myself from those bloodsuckers."

CJ looked at her watch. Time passed more quickly than she realized. Luckily, the zig-zagging stroll brought her to within twenty yards of the row that marked the final resting place of June Harper-Quisenheimer. CJ looked to the entrance and saw the personal truck of Ranger Quint Fowler pull under the metal archway. She chewed her lower lip and walked to the pre-arranged spot. The prayers that came so easily a few moments ago failed her as the truck crept to a stop.

The door opened and the man in the passenger seat

thanked Quint with a voice that sounded alarmingly familiar. He turned and looked down to where his foot would land.

Looking up and into her her father-in-law's eyes, CJ gasped. Except for two inches of height, gray around the temples, and a face creased with age, she saw her husband.

Mumbled, confused words ran through her mind. Not knowing how to address him or what he wanted to call her, she settled for a pinched smile.

Misty eyes looked into CJ's as she hugged her elbows across the middle of her body. He stuffed sunglasses into a shirt pocket and took three steps toward her. "You remind me of June. When she was nervous, her tongue tied in knots a sailor couldn't untangle." He paused and extended a hand for her to clasp. "If it's all the same to you, I'll call you Catherine. Why don't you call me Bob, or Dad? It's your choice."

CJ bypassed his hand and filled his arms. "I'd prefer Dad, if you don't mind."

"Where's David?"

"Close. He moves around like a ghost when he wants to. He's watching us."

Bob shook his head. "He loved to sneak up on his mother and scare the living daylights out of her."

"Hi, Dad. I see you met CJ." The two look-a-likes embraced. CJ searched for a tissue. As usual, she came up short and had to use a shirt sleeve.

Husband and wife walked on each side of Bob as they approached the headstone. Its modest size brought a wave of guilt.

"Dad, we can have this replaced with something bigger."

Bob's head swayed back and forth like a playground swing coming to a stop. "There's no need. She's not here."

CJ handed her father-in-law a single rose. "I brought this for you to give to June." Her voice cracked like thin china when she tried to say more.

Silence enveloped the area. Bob fell to his knees and allowed grief to pour forth.

Robert's farewell to his wife needed to be spoken in private, so CJ and David eased away.

Quint's approach caused David and CJ to move toward the grave. "Dad, we need to be going, it's not safe here," said David.

Bob rose, wiped his cheeks, and turned to face his new life.

"Thanks, this meant so much to me." Final hugs ended the mini-reunion. CJ's father-in-law cast his gaze to David and asked, "Are you sure you two can't come with me today?"

David's head moved left to right. "We have things to do for Monday. Biff and I will be out tomorrow." David paused and stared at a city police car that passed the cemetery. He relaxed when the car sped away with emergency lights on. "The sheriff knows who I am and that I'm here for the reunion. We don't want to give him cause to think anything else. It's best we split up today. We're too close to the end to be making mistakes."

"My goodness. You have grown up."

Biff's pickup, trailer and boat entered through the gate and stopped near the gravesite. Bob climbed in.

With his ever-present smile, Biff said, "Hey, Mr. Q. Long time, no see. I brought you a present." He handed Bob a baseball cap, complete with bushy blond fake hair protruding from the sides and a pony tail dangling from the back. "No one will recognize you with this on."

Bob put on the hat and added the wrap-around sunglasses. "Did you happen to bring that can of vanishing powder I gave you?"

Biff struck the steering wheel with an open palm and laughed loud enough to scare a nearby bird. "I bow to the champion of practical jokes."

"You'd better be going," said David. "I'll see you tomorrow, Dad."

Biff made a quick exit. Quint delayed leaving until Biff's pickup, boat and trailer approached the gate. CJ and David headed for the mini-van but spun around at the sight of three sheriff's department cars flying into position. One pulled Biff over while two others swung into the cemetery, cutting off Quint.

CJ's heart tattooed a rapid beat. David held her arm when she tried to break toward the minivan. "Wait! No fast moves."

The scene played out in front of them like a silent movie. Two officers approached Biff's truck, one on the driver's side and one on the passenger's. Quint exited his truck with badge in one hand and gun-hand empty. His raised voice could be heard but not understood from where they stood.

Once again CJ focused on Biff's truck. The officer on the passenger side motioned to the one talking to Biff. He issued an impatient wave. The truck inched away from the curb.

"They made it!" exclaimed CJ.

Sweat dripped from David's chin. He looked at his forearm. "Do you think you could retract your claws?" Five deep divots showed when CJ surrendered her grip.

The two sheriff's office cars pulled around Quint and came their way. They turned on the row before June's grave, giving hard stares out of closed windows.

"Just as well," said David. "I don't think I could have stopped myself if they'd said anything."

CJ tugged David's shirt. "Come on, Rambo. Dad's safe and we have the day to ourselves."

Twenty minutes later David received a text that brought a smile to his face. He showed the screen to CJ.

Boat in water. Mr. Q told cops he needed burial plot for pet racoon. Hat, wig and sunglasses did the trick.

CHAPTER THIRTY-ONE

A late morning swim followed by room service and a decent nap left CJ rested and alert. She examined herself in the mirror and nodded with approval. Two hours of sunshine gave her skin a healthy glow. The daily two-mile runs she'd committed to had also worked their magic. The black sleeveless dress would do nicely for tonight.

She applied more than the usual amount of makeup. Instead of the normal free-flowing hair, she decided on a casual up-do. This might be the only time she'd ever see some of these people, but she wanted to look her best.

Removing the black dress from the hanger, she stepped into it. Turning her back to David she asked, "Could you help me with the zipper?"

"This looks like a one-way zipper. It only goes down."

"Up, now. Down, later."

David trilled his tongue, making the sound of a purring tiger. Placing his hands on her shoulders, he turned her for inspection. "Wow." A light kiss found its way to that special spot on her neck. "Do we have to go to the reunion?" he whispered.

She moved to arm's length to catch her breath. "I couldn't help but notice you in the pool today, Mr. Harper. Have you been hitting the gym?"

David scooped her in his arms and delivered a kiss that made his desire for her abundantly clear.

She managed a breathless whisper. "Biff and Amy are downstairs at the restaurant waiting on us."

"Who cares about food?" Another kiss followed. CJ felt her defenses and knees weaken.

A ring tone playing circus music cut through the hotel room. "Saved by the bell," said CJ.

"Only a temporary reprieve."

David picked up his phone. "Hey, Biff. We'll be right down."

The hotel boasted a four-star restaurant with an award-winning chef. Walking in the wake of a willowy hostess, Biff pretended to whisper. His words carried for several yards.

The hostess looked down to see if her blouse buttons were all joined. "Coach Stewart, you get me with that every time. Mrs. Stewart, how do you put up with him?"

Amy allowed a smile to answer for her. She wore her hair piled on her head with two lacquered chop sticks protruding from the red mound. As usual, she wore a dress buttoned all the way to the throat. Tonight, however, University of Arkansas red shimmered with every step.

A waiter came to take drink orders. "Iced tea here and here," David pointed to his place and CJ's.

"I'll take a draft beer in an ice-cold mug," said Biff. "What do you want, honey?"

"Water with lemon. I may take a sip of your beer."

Biff raised his eyebrows. "This is going to be a good night. I can feel it all the way down to my dancing shoes."

Amy giggled at the inside joke.

CJ dismissed it and asked, "How is your room?"

"It's wonderful," Amy released a huge sigh.

The waiter delivered drinks. Amy reached for Biff's beer before he could get his hand off the table. She didn't put the bottle down until she'd downed a quarter of it.

Biff's smile broadened.

Instead of a heavy meal, the foursome ordered three samplings of decadent appetizers. Biff replenished his beer and managed to drink most of it before Amy polished it off. She released the top button of her dress and looked at David. "I heard you had some excitement this morning at the cemetery."

A bead of condensation slid down David's glass of iced tea. "I thought I'd lost dad again." He looked up and smiled. "That goofy hat saved the day. I called Quint this afternoon. He said dad found a sketch pad and went to work on a pencil drawing of the bay."

The class clown wasn't smiling. "That little stunt by the sheriff's deputies this morning scared me out of a few years of my life."

"With any luck, that will be the last excitement we'll have on this trip," said CJ.

Biff looked at his cell phone and pushed back his chair. "The reunion starts in three minutes. I'll ruin my reputation if I'm not the first to arrive and the last to leave."

THE FIRST HOUR of the reunion passed at the pace of a sloth. CJ nodded, smiled and shook hands with David's classmates and their spouses or dates.

"I don't recognize half these people," said David. "I can't believe how much they've changed. Some of the studs are duds."

CJ countered with, "I bet some of the girls that were wall-flowers look like a million dollars."

"Oh, no," said David. "Speaking of girls changing, there's Charlie."

CJ made a half-turn and spied David's ex-flame wobble. "She must have started early on the mixed drinks." A bejeweled index finger poked Amy. "David, this could get ugly. You'd better break them up."

"What do you want me to do?" He sounded like a helpless ninth grader.

"Ask Charlie to dance. That'll give Amy a chance to get away before she punches her out."

"Ugh. I'll do it, but I won't like it."

CJ watched as David strode to where both women stood with hands on hips. He stepped between them. Biff sidled up next to CJ and joined his gaze with hers. "You're spoiling my fun. That red-haired spitfire I'm married to isn't going to take much more." Biff raised his hand as if he would salute, but passed it in front of his nose. "Amy's had it up to here with that heifer."

DAVID DID his best to keep his distance on the dance floor, but Charlene had other ideas. The slow ballad of lost love was the excuse she needed to hold him close. Halfway through the song she laid her head on his chest and purred, "I knew you'd make your move."

Huh? Make his move? He wanted to move, all right. Move as fast as he could out of her clutches.

"Last night I saw you looking at me. You were remembering the old times, weren't you?" Charlene stumbled. David silently berated his cat-like reflexes as soon as he caught her.

She used the opportunity to coo and press herself even closer against him. "How can we do this and not get caught?"

"Do what?"

"You're right. We need to whisper. I'll get my business card and slip it in your pocket." She turned her head and released a belch that reeked of fruity rum and lasagna.

David did his best to blow the stench away. Charlene continued as if nothing had happened. "My number is on the card. Send me a text later on. I'll get a room."

David jerked his head around and spied Biff. He mouthed a single word. "Help!"

Biff looked briefly at CJ. "Every time I turn around, I have to pull your husband out of a jam." He strode to a table topped with platters of finger foods and grabbed two baby carrots. Slipping them under his top lip created two orange fangs. People began to giggle when Biff slouched and swung his arms wide like a gorilla. He walked across the dance floor and stood behind Charlie so David could see him. The dancers stopped, and the room rocked with laughter as the class clown reprised a role he played in high school.

David couldn't help himself. He, too, grabbed his knees and bellowed.

"What is it?" asked Charlie. "Why is everyone laughing?"

She turned and came face to face with the orange-fanged gorilla. An open palm swung. Biff saw it coming in plenty of time and stepped back. Like a cartoon hippo wearing a tutu, Charlie missed the target, turned a pirouette, and landed in a heap. David offered a hand to the crimson-faced woman, but received a cussing instead. He made a hasty retreat to the refuge of CJ's outstretched hand.

"I'm going to the men's room. If Charlie comes anywhere near me the rest of the night, shoot her," said David.

CJ covered her mouth to muffle the laugh. Amy joined her with a half-empty bottle of beer clutched in her hand. With yet another button unhooked she tilted the bottle to the ceiling.

CHAPTER THIRTY-TWO

I n the men's restroom, David washed his face and hands. He wished he could wash away the memory of a dance gone horribly bad. In walked Stephen Shipley.

"David, I'm glad you're here. There's something I want to say to you."

"Oh?" David braced for another onslaught by the husband of the woman who'd propositioned him a few minutes ago.

With head bowed, the assistant district attorney hesitated. "I want to apologize." He lifted his gaze and gained eye contact. "I was way out of line yesterday. Can we find a place to talk?"

Confused by the sudden change, David said, "How about the lobby? There's a nice sitting area out there."

The two made their way to the overgrown planter box. David took a chair while Stephen sat on the edge of the love seat, almost knee to knee.

"Where to start? This past year has been terrible," Stephen said.

Could this be the beginning of a real confession? David

leaned forward. "Why don't you start back in high school? That's when things fell apart between us."

"You're right. We worked so hard for three years to have a winning team. Can you imagine how many passes I threw to you and Biff? He had hands like glue, but you were something special. With both of you running patterns we could've gone all the way in the playoffs. Back then, I believed if I could lead a team to the state championship, I'd be on my way to the top of whatever I wanted to do. Then...you were gone."

"One receiver, double-covered every play. That's all you had our senior year," said David.

Stephen's head nodded in agreement. "That wasn't the worst of it. The heart and soul of the team left when you did. What happened to your folks made football petty. We fell apart." Stephen looked at his shoes. "I hated you."

"And now?"

"Now?" Stephen's gaze came back to David. "Now I find I've wasted some of the best years of my life. It's time for changes."

David leaned back and made a steeple of his fingers. "What kind of changes?"

Stephen looked toward the ballroom. "Charlie and I are through. I moved out a month ago." An irony-filled laugh slipped out. "I moved out after I felt the boot on my backside. It didn't take Daddy Rhoades long to have a restraining order put on me. Charlie filed for divorce even before she threw me out. In case you didn't notice, I've been keeping my distance from her."

"I'm sorry." David knew he didn't sound convincing.

"Don't be. I'm not sure what she and her daddy and the sheriff are up to, but it's not good." With voice lowered he continued, "No one can live the way those three do and not be crooked as a drunk snake."

"Oh?"

"You work with the Rangers. You're bound to know a lot more than I do about the mess with your dad. The DA kept me in the dark."

David did some fishing. "Are you saying the DA isn't a crook?"

The response came immediately. "He's a jerk that believes once someone is found guilty, that's the end of the story. He's also smart. He knows every legal trick there is to delay appeals."

Stephen turned his head to look away. "That dressing down Lucy and Arlene gave me yesterday hit home. I had a sleepless night, and I've been thinking all day. I bought the lie that says the adversarial system of law is more important than the truth. They drilled that into my head so much at law school that I came to believe it. For years I stood by and watched my boss do everything possible to try to keep your dad in prison. For what? It didn't have anything to do with justice."

He moved back on the love seat. "Did you catch the news last night? That was justice. I deserved every one of the phone calls I got today. You should've heard what the DA called me."

David nodded. "It sounds like you're at a crossroads, not only in your personal life, but in your career, too."

"You always were a smart guy. I'll be in court Monday morning at your dad's hearing. The district attorney doesn't want his face associated with the case now that it's lost. As soon as the hearing is finished, I'm turning in my resignation. I might as well get it in before the DA can fire me. I never did like criminal law."

"Why'd you do it? There are so many other areas of law you could practice."

Stephen hung his head. "I married Charlie because her daddy said he'd put me on the fast track to a political career.

Boy, did that backfire. He got me into the DA's office and used me as his spy. Every Sunday Charlie and I went to his home for lunch. For two or three hours he'd grill me on everything going on in the DA's office."

David's eyes darted as his mind raced to process the implications of what Stephen told him. "What are you going to do?"

Stephen leaned back and his expression brightened. "I started putting feelers out a few weeks ago. Something told me my days at the DA's office were about over. I have a new job waiting on me."

The music in the ballroom stopped. A man's muddled voice filtered into the lobby. Stephen rose and extended a hand. "I wanted to tell you I'm sorry for being such a jerk. I hope we can leave here as friends again."

David rose, clasped the extended hand, and pulled Stephen in for a gentle slap on the back. "All is forgiven." He hesitated. "Stephen, can I give you some advice?"

"Sure, I need all the help I can get."

"Lose the comb over. Get the sides high and tight. You'll be surprised how many women like a man who's confident in himself."

"Thanks. The only reason I wear it this way is because Charlie insisted on it."

"Let's go. I'll introduce you to the best thing that ever happened to me."

David approached his wife with his arm draped over Shipwreck Shipley's shoulder. After introductions, Stephen excused himself to get a celebratory drink.

CJ pulled on the lapel of David's coat. He dipped his ear toward her mouth. "Tonight is like reading *Alice in Wonderland*. Things are getting curiouser and curiouser."

"WHO'S the guy with the microphone?" asked CJ.

"That's Brian Boxwhite, our class president. The people that are coming on stage are the other class officers."

CJ watched a string of women climb the three steps to the small platform. Snickers followed gasps as the class treasurer, Charlene Rhoades-Shipley, didn't lift her foot high enough to clear the last step. If the class president hadn't been there to catch her, she would have plowed into the drum set.

"She's plastered again." Stephen wagged his head as a mixture of pity and disdain filled his voice.

Decorum prevailed, and Brian thanked everyone for attending. The class secretary stepped to his side with a stack of framed award certificates. One by one, Brian gave out awards for the alumnus who had traveled the farthest, the least changed, the most children, and other good-natured forms of recognition. The next award went to the alumnus who'd lost the most hair.

"Stephen Shipley, come up and receive the coveted Cue Ball Award," announced Brian Boxwhite.

Stephen howled with laughter as he climbed the stairs. He swept past a teetering Charlie and moved to receive his award. He reached into a coat pocket, produced a comb and swept back the comb-over blond locks. He bent forward for the crowd to see and used an index finger to point to his shining scalp. The room exploded in applause.

"I can get rid of that." The voice came from the right side of the room where a woman held up a pair of scissors.

David leaned into CJ. "That's Sissy McBride. At least that's her maiden name. She received her cosmetology training in high school. Biff said she owns a shop in Clute."

Chants of "Cut it off" rang through the crowd. Stephen beckoned Sissy to come and shear him. A chair found its way on stage and in a few minutes the attorney beamed almost as brightly as his emancipated head.

Stephen received back slaps and a fair amount of lip-shaped red smears on his cranium as he worked his way back to David and CJ.

CJ jerked her head up as a shriek pierced the room. "WOOO...PIG...SOOIE!"

Instead of the call coming from Biff, a small-framed, red-headed woman stood with hands megaphoned around her mouth.

Biff leaped onto the stage, cupped a hand behind an ear and leaned forward as if straining to catch a distant sound.

Amy repeated the call. "WOOO...PIG...SOOIE!"

Biff moved in front of the lead singer and spoke into the microphone. "Make a path folks. It's time to party!"

The crowd parted. Amy kicked off her high heels, jerked the chop sticks from the pile of red hair, and cast them aside. With the steps of a gymnast she ran forward, performed a round off, completed two back handsprings and ended the run with a perfect back flip with a half twist. After a spot-on landing she tossed a mountain of hair from her face, crouched, and pointed at her husband. "Tell that band to get after it."

Biff turned to the lead guitarist. "Hit it, boys." The guitar riff of a hard-driving country-rock song that topped the charts fifteen years earlier filled the room.

With the skill of a dancer from an NFL cheerleader squad, Amy danced, kicked, shook, shimmied and mesmerized the crowd. Biff jumped from the stage and joined his wife in a gyrating dance that brought applause and shouts of approval.

"Good grief," said CJ. "If Herod's stepdaughter could dance like Amy, there's no wonder he promised her half his kingdom. I've never seen anything like it."

"Yeah," David squeaked out, his eyes and mouth in a contest to see which could open the widest.

Stephen Shipley leaned into them and shouted over the music. "Amy was a gymnast in college. They only do this once every five years at the reunion. It's why so many people came this year. Keep watching and join in when everyone else does."

The first verse came to an end. Amy shifted gears as the familiar chorus produced a sing-along from the crowd. Biff stood and raised his arms in the air. Quick motions beckoned all to join in. Everyone, save the sullen and inebriated Charlene Rhoades-Shipley, filled the room with every sort of dance imaginable.

David looked at CJ and shrugged. "When in Rome..." They could hardly move due to laughter and the sea of people. The song ended, and the party moved into high gear.

Brian Boxwhite, the class president turned banker, handed David a sealed envelope. "I'll be in my office on Monday morning if anyone needs to talk to me."

David thrust the letter in his coat pocket and gave a sincere, "Thank you."

The band played an extra set at no charge. Worth it, and then some, to watch Amy dance.

CHAPTER THIRTY-THREE

CJ sent shoes flying when they reached their room. "Remind me to never again dance in heels. My dogs are barking like they've been chasing rabbits."

David took off his jacket and wiggled out of the shoulder holster.

"What's in that letter Brian gave you?" asked CJ.

"I almost forgot." David pulled out a pocket knife and cut along the top crease. "It's a copy of a legal document signed by Judge Rhoades." David sat at the desk, turned on the lamp and carefully read. "It's a court order that names Charlene as the conservator over Dad's estate."

CJ's mouth twisted before she asked, "The judge named his daughter to watch over your parents' estate? Why would he do that?"

David stood and began to pace. "Don't you see? This gave him access to all of Mom and Dad's possessions, including bank accounts and safe deposit boxes." David snapped his fingers. "So that's what happened to all the money."

"What do you mean?"

"Uncle Ray tried to get access to Mom and Dad's bank

accounts. I wasn't on the signature cards and the bank needed a court order instructing them what to do."

"I don't understand."

"Judge Rhoades was the DA during Dad's trial. The sentencing judge retired a month later. The trial took place in October and elections are held in November. Uncle Ray got sick and gave up trying to be named executor of the estate. I focused on getting into the Army and leaving the past behind. I put the money in their account out of my mind until years later. By then, Uncle Ray had died, and I tried to forget all about my prior life.

"Look at the date." David pointed to a line on the page. "Judge Rhoades issued this order three years after he took office. He waited until Charlene turned twenty-one. With no one to petition the court or hound the bank, the money stayed where it was."

"For three years?"

David snapped his fingers. "I bet if we do a records search, we'll find the judge named himself as executor soon after his election. He took the extra step to get it out of his name as soon as Charlene reached her majority."

CJ sat on the bed and propped herself up with pillows. She folded another pillow in half and slid it under her feet. "What happened to the money?" Her eyebrows pinched together. "Wait a minute, if Charlene took the money and they used it themselves, that's illegal."

David paced and nodded. "That's right. But it could also be they never touched the money. They might've added to it." David's eyes darted back and forth. "They could have kept the savings and checking accounts open and stored things in the safe deposit boxes. It would still be under Mom and Dad's names, but they'd have full access to them."

David stopped in mid-pace and lowered his voice. "Of course. That's it!"

CJ almost shouted when David remained silent. "What? What's it?"

"That's why they want to kill Dad. They're afraid he'll go looking for his money. It's only natural Dad will check on his accounts after his release."

David moved toward the bed and sat on the edge facing CJ. "Judge Rhoades is a very clever man. He's covered his tracks by involving middle men in his illegal projects. He also found a way to stash the illegally obtained money."

"Don't forget Charlie."

David nodded.

"Do you have enough for a warrant?"

"I don't know." He waved the papers. "I'll give this to Quint tomorrow morning."

CJ yawned. "Speaking of morning, it's almost 2:00 a.m."

"You're right." David looked at his watch. "It'll be a short night for Biff and me. We're heading out before first light. You'd better get some sleep if you're coming with us."

"About that...Go to the bay house without me. It sounds like an all boy party since Amy can't go. Besides, Dotty and Jessica are coming for the hearing. I think we'll relax by the pool."

"Ah-ha. Now we're getting to the truth." David leaned over and nibbled below her ear. "You want to lounge with Dotty and Jessica after you sleep late." Soft kisses worked their way to CJ's mouth. He began another sentence, but she cut him off.

"Don't you think you've talked long enough?"

CHAPTER THIRTY-FOUR

David secured the bow of the aluminum flat-bottom boat while Biff attached the stern. "Good morning," rang out from the deck above. "It looks like you two survived the reunion."

David squinted into a blue sky. "Good morning, Dad. You may be only half right. I'm not sure about Biff. He started off grumpy this morning and hasn't improved a bit."

"What's wrong, Biff? Too much of a good thing?"

Biff scowled and trudged up the stairs behind David, who carried an assortment of sacks.

The class clown found his voice when he reached the deck. "Must have coffee. I can't function without coffee."

"Dad, I'm putting your clothes for tomorrow on the bed in the corner."

The resurrected ancient percolator once again performed its duty. David poured them each a mug, and they joined Bob and Quint on the deck. Lapping waters and screeching sea gulls filled the air with sounds that had been a big part of his young life.

Bob waited until Biff finished most of his first mug before

he asked, "Are you going to tell us why you have the mulli-grubs or not?"

Biff gazed across the shimmering waters of the bay. "I had a perfect night planned. Amy couldn't have been in a better mood. We danced and danced. She looked great. I couldn't wait to get back to the room." Biff looked back from the horizon to Bob and exclaimed, "I even bought flowers and put petals on the sheets."

Bob nodded, but said nothing.

"The chair. That darn chair in the lobby." Biff hung his head and wagged it back and forth. "We walked to the lobby on our way to the elevator. Amy left her shoes and those silly chop-sticks she had in her hair back in the ballroom. She sat down and told me to go find them." Biff looked up through eyes pleading for understanding. "I couldn't have been gone but a few minutes. When I got back, she might as well have been comatose." Biff gave a final sigh. "I threw her over my shoulder and took her up to the room. Right about now she's waking up looking for the cat that slept in her mouth, and making some sort of vow never to book another hotel room."

With tongue firmly planted in his cheek, Bob rose with a coffee mug lifted high in a salute. "To love!"

Three more mugs rose skyward to join the salute. "Love!"

Biff retreated to his sulking and David handed Quint the order signed by Judge Rhoades. Quint read it twice, handed it to Bob and looked off in the distance. When Bob finished reading it, he handed it back to Quint without comment.

Quint broke the silence. "What do you think, David?"

"It could go either way. If it were anyone but a state district judge, we'd have plenty to get an arrest warrant right now. We need to speak to the special prosecutor and Brian Boxwhite first. It would probably be better if the special prosecutor asked for a search warrant, or at least a subpoena. Besides, the bank won't open until tomorrow morning and we have plenty to keep us busy. I gave Brian my card. He told me he'd call if anything unusual happens tomorrow morning."

Quint nodded in agreement. "Slow and sure usually wins the race."

Bob stood and looked over the rail at calm waters. He took in a deep breath of air that carried the scent of brine-infused water and salt grass. "I've been working on this forgiveness thing for quite some time. I've come to a conclusion. It's going to be a lot easier to forgive these people once they're in a cell like the one they put me in."

David rose and stood by his father with one hand on his shoulder. "Dad, let's go fishing."

"I can't."

"Why not?"

"No license. I might get a ticket."

Quint chuckled. Biff choked on his coffee. David patted his dad between his shoulder blades. "Between Quint and me, we should be able to talk the game warden out of giving you a ticket."

"WE'RE HERE." The voice of Dotty Sylvester brought a smile to CJ's face. "We can't get in our room yet. Can we hang out in yours until they let us check in?"

"Come on up. I'm in 417. Bring your bags. You can change here and we can go to the pool."

Familiar muffled voices had CJ on her feet and at the door before Dotty and Jessica could knock. Squeals of greeting bounced down the hallway. With their suitcases tucked into a corner, Dotty nudged Jessica. "Go ahead. Show her."

The Venus of Agape Christian University held out a model's left hand. On it sparkled a ring with a solitaire diamond.

CJ reached for the ring and sputtered, "Oh, my gosh. It's beautiful. When did he ask you? Where were you? Tell me all about it."

Jessica pushed a mass of soft reddish-blond hair over her shoulder and began. "Bea and Billy Paul asked Mark and me to supper yesterday. After we ate, she told the funniest story of how Billy Paul asked her to marry him. I almost wet my pants I laughed so hard. Anyway, when we left, Mark parked in the middle of the concrete bridge that crosses over the river at their house. That's where he asked me."

CJ didn't let on that David had chosen the same spot to propose to her after a similar experience at Casa Stargate. "That sounds perfect. Have you told your parents?"

Jessica nodded. "I Skyped with Mom and Dad last night. They're thrilled."

CJ shifted her gaze to Dotty. "Are you two hungry?"

"We had a late breakfast. What we really want is to get some sunshine. You said the pool is nice?"

"This is a new hotel. Everything is nice. Let's get our swim suits on and check it out."

Chatting like hens clucking, the three strode out a glass door and headed to the kidney-shaped pool. As usual, all heads turned to watch Jessica cross the patio. And, as usual, she had not a clue. CJ pinned her hair up and lay back on the lounger. A good husband, an unexpected father-in-law and friends you could count on. What more could I ask for?

CJ turned her head toward Dotty. "Is everything ready for tomorrow?"

"Every television station and newspaper you can name will be there. If all goes well, we'll have a video of everything and everyone. It's going to be tricky, but I spoke with Quint and we worked out a plan." Dotty gazed at CJ through sunglasses and giggled. "After that clip with you and David being hand-cuffed went viral, this court proceeding is page one."

"The what?"

"The viral video. One of the three people that filmed you in handcuffs put what they recorded on several social media sites."

"Biff Stewart," whispered CJ.

Dotty continued. "This has turned into a national story. I never could've generated this much heat on the judge and sheriff by myself. Thanks for making my job so easy."

Sarcasm dripped from CJ's words. "Glad I could be of some small assistance."

The three women rotated like chickens on a spit. CJ and Jessica had their heads turned so they faced each other. "Did you bring the makeup kit?" asked CJ.

"It's in the room. I'll put the skills I learned in theater class to work. I hope I remember how to apply it properly."

"I'm sure you'll do fine." A drop of stinging sweat rolled into CJ's eye. "I don't know about you chicks, but this hen needs to cool off."

The two women joined her as she rose and moved toward the shallow end of the pool. A man, apparently headed for the fitness room, took a shortcut through the pool area. With his gaze locked on the three women, he stepped into the deep end without breaking stride.

Laughing, CJ turned to Jessica. "Don't you get tired of men staring at you?"

A coy smile crossed the co-ed's face. "He was looking at Dotty."

"No way," replied the trim, petite blond. "He couldn't take his eyes off CJ. Look at her. She's fit and there's a glow about her that could roast marshmallows."

In unison the trio spoke over each other as they pointed, defended their choice, splashed, and laughed. For a while CJ lost track of time and the serious task that lay before her. How good to have friends, but they could only do so much.

CHAPTER THIRTY-FIVE

The outboard motor sputtered to a stop after David hit the kill switch. Two miles from the elevated house with the clown face, father and son baited hooks and tossed lines into salty water. Guided only by tide and a slight breeze, the boat crept across the expanse of water. Shrimp attached to treble hooks drifted four feet under white corks with red hats.

"I wish we had live shrimp instead of these frozen ones," said David.

Bob took in a full breath of freedom. "These will do fine, son." He gazed at a crane as it skimmed the water and caught a small fish. "Just fine."

Twenty minutes of fishing resulted in not even the slightest dip of a cork. David reeled in his line, removed the cork, re-baited the hook with a more promising specimen and tossed it back in. He felt the lead weight skip across the sandy bottom as the shrimp trailed nine inches behind.

"You must be after flounder," said Bob.

"Yeah, it looks like nothing else is going to bite. One of those flat fish may be nestled down in the sand."

"You might be right, but I'll stay up higher. Did you see the mullet working a few minutes ago? That's usually a good sign. We should be right over them."

Bob's cork dove out of sight, his pole jerked and thrashed.

"Hang onto him, Dad. Work him slow. You might need to take a little drag off. Don't let him break the line."

Bob looked at David and let out a huff of exasperation. "This isn't my first time, son. In fact, if I remember correctly, I taught you how to land a fish."

David nodded at the fatherly reprimand as he reached for the landing net. In no time, Bob ran a stringer through the lower lip of a four-pound speckled trout. Three more of similar size joined the first before the school moved on.

"Do you want to chase the mullet and get some more, Dad?"

"No, this'll be plenty for tonight. I'll take the hook off and watch the cork."

"I'll reel mine in," said David.

Time passed in solitude as new bonds formed without words. A passing boat, going at full bore, rocked their small boat and broke Bob's trance.

"Son."

"Yes, sir?"

"What did it take to change your name?"

A wave of trepidation crossed David's mind. "Are you angry that I changed my name?"

"Heavens no. I'm sorry if you got that impression. The only reason I'm asking is because I need to do the same thing."

David turned his head to look eye to eye with his father. "Why would you want to do that?"

Bob reeled in his line as he explained. "As long as my last name is Quisenheimer, I'll be known as either the man who murdered his wife, or the man wrongly convicted of murdering his wife. I won't be seen as anything else. It might take a while, but with a new last name, I'll stand a better chance of being known for just being me."

David nodded. "I see what you mean." It occurred to him he'd changed his name for the same reason.

After a short pause, David answered the original question. "It's not hard. You don't have to have a lawyer, but I'd recommend you get one. All you do is petition the court, wait a while, go to a hearing, and it's done. No big deal. What last names are you considering?"

"Only one. Harper."

David swallowed hard as his father continued. "Your mother took my mouthful of a last name and wore it proudly. The least I can do is follow the footsteps of my son and take her name. Besides, it'll be much less confusing for everyone that knows you and Catherine. I'm going to start using it as soon as we get to Riverview. That way people won't have to learn one name and relearn another."

David plunged his hand in a small blue ice chest and pulled out a bottle of water. "We'll get it taken care of as quick as we can."

Bob broke the pleasant silence when David removed his hat and raked his left hand through his hair. "What's on your mind, son?"

"Why do you ask?"

"You ran your left hand through your hair. You never did that unless you'd done something wrong or wanted to ask for something you knew you shouldn't."

"Remind me not to play poker with you."

David paused for several seconds, screwed up his courage and asked a question he hoped would not reopen a sewn-up wound. "I have my suspicions about who killed Mom. We know that convict Barcroft participated, but someone else had a hand in it. Who do you suspect?"

Without emotion or hesitation Bob answered, "First, I'd like to hear your theory."

The words spilled out. "The sheriff. I can't prove it, but I believe the DNA on the other knife belongs to him."

"That doesn't make sense," said Bob as he retrieved a bottle of water. "All members of law enforcement have their DNA on file. That way, if they work a crime scene and inadvertently contaminate it, they can be ruled out as suspects. The sheriff worked the case, but his DNA didn't match what they found on the knife."

"Think again, Dad," replied David in a soft voice. "Answer me two questions: First, when did the sheriff give his DNA sample?"

"I don't know. I'm sure different departments vary across the state and nation. It probably was dependent on when they had the money to do it."

David answered his own question. "Twenty years ago, the Brazoria County Sheriff's Department made DNA testing mandatory." He paused and allowed the statement to sink in. "Here's the most important question. Who collected the DNA for the sheriff's department?"

Bob's eyes widened. His fists tightened, then loosened. "The sheriff. He'd be the ultimate authority to verify who the samples from his department came from."

"You're almost correct. The sheriff, or his designee. The current sheriff wasn't elected until eighteen years ago, but he worked in the sheriff's department when the samples were taken. I'll bet your gold magnet the sheriff designated him to oversee the taking of samples. He could've taken a swab from anyone, alive or dead, and put his name on it."

A plan leaped into David's mind and he moved to start the engine. "Let's get back to the bay house. I need to do a little detective work and pay the sheriff a late-night visit."

CHAPTER THIRTY-SIX

The mini-van slowed enough to facilitate David's exit. He crouched low, duck-walked to a barbed wire fence and slithered between two of the strands. Creeping into a tree-studded field, he moved quick and sure. Cattle lay quietly off to his right, bedded down for the night under the outstretched branches of a mature stand of pecan trees.

By studying Google satellite maps he and CJ got the lay of the land. More information had been gathered by driving past the road that separated Judge Rhoades' estate from the smaller, yet substantial, home and land belonging to the sheriff.

Dressed in black, his face painted with green stripes over a black base, David moved from shadow to shadow with such stealth the locusts didn't interrupt their symphony. He stopped at the last tree before reaching a white wooden fence. A driveway, shaped like a paper clip, stretched in front the sheriff's ranch style home.

He reached into the pocket of black cargo pants and retrieved the inexpensive walkie-talkie, bought solely for this occasion. "I'm at the circular drive. No lights on inside. There must be a dog with a shock collar. I see little posts sticking up, the kind used for an invisible fence. At least he won't be able to get me once I'm back on this side. Wish me luck."

"I'll pray instead."

David moved forward, placed a right hand on the top rail of the fence and, in a singular motion, leaped over. Once again in a crouch, he waited to make sure he'd not been detected as a light breeze helped cool his accumulating perspiration. The sheriff's patrol car sat broadside in front of him. The hum of the home's air conditioner muffled most noises, save the chatter of insects. Then, all went graveyard quiet.

David waited for the compressor and fan to cycle on again before he sprinted to the car. He ducked below the window and tested the driver's door. It sprang open. The dome light threw a pie-shaped slice of light onto the grass behind him. "Nice of the sheriff to leave it unlocked." In no time he pulled the fuse to the dome light. For the next five minutes he wiped sweat from stinging eyes as he completed his night's work.

He gave his surroundings a good long look. *Thirty yards and I'll be in the clear.*

The air conditioner continued to hum as David slid from the front seat. "So far, so good." His gloved hand slipped as he pushed the car door. He tried to catch it, but couldn't. The clunk of a closing car door echoed through the night air a full second after the air conditioner cut off.

Angry baritone barks erupted from the back of the house. David sprang from his crouch like a sprinter coming out of starting blocks. "Big dog!" he yelped as the vigilant K9 closed the distance. He approached the fence at full speed and dove head first over the wooden barricade, tucked and somersaulted. He came up on his feet and stumbled forward. David was aware of three sounds—the skidding of the guard dog as it attempted to stop, a painful yelp, and a squishing noise when he hit the ground.

He sprinted another eighth of a mile before ducking behind a tree. The dog continued his frustrated declarations, but they brought no response from the house.

"Come and get me." David slid the yellow and black radio into one of several pockets on his pants and navigated the remaining distance. Frozen in place behind a last tree before the fence, he waited until the mini-van's headlights came into view. A push down on the third strand of barbed wire and a skilled step freed him of the property boundary and a trespassing charge. Squatting in the ditch, he peeled off his shirt, turned it inside out, and wadded it into a ball. He waited for the van to stop before he jerked open the door and plopped in the passenger seat.

"Get us out of here."

CJ clothespinned her nose with her thumb and index finger. "What's that smell? Have you been rolling in a feed lot?"

"I had to take a flying leap over a fence and landed on a fresh meadow muffin. Stop at the first place you see and I'll throw this shirt away."

CJ giggled at her husband's plight as she rolled down her window. "Other than that, did you get everything hooked up?"

"The trap is set."

CJ glanced into a field as the moon illuminated the landscape of the judge's property. "There's the runway for the judge's airplane. It looks longer at night than it did this afternoon."

"With any luck he'll never use it again."

CHAPTER THIRTY-SEVEN

Dotty, Jessica and CJ hovered over David as he sat with a towel draped around his neck. CJ opened the lap-top computer, pulled up a day-old photo of her father-in-law and put it where Jessica could see. She opened a box of theatrical makeup and declared, "Here goes. Let's see how much you remember." The process of adding twenty years to David's appearance began.

First, Jessica applied foundation to match skin tone. "No, a little lighter," said Dotty. "Bob's been inside for years."

Laugh lines and wrinkles appeared with the stroke of a fine-tipped brush. Gray powder lightened the hair around the temples. The addition of black-frame glasses served to distract from the face.

"Not bad at all," whispered CJ. "This will work."

Dotty nodded as Jessica added a final furrow to David's forehead. CJ gave her approval but then grimaced. "Remember to slouch and bend your knees. We can't do anything about the height except put your dad in shoes with lifts."

"I don't see how you women can stand to smear this paint

on every day." David stood and examined his transformed face in the mirror. "It looks good until you get close."

Dotty peeled the towel away from David's neck. "Things will be moving fast. I can't see how anyone will be able to tell you and your dad apart." She looked at her watch. "It's seven-thirty. I need to get going. I told the news crews to be ready for action at eight-thirty. They're meeting me at the courthouse."

"Perfect," said David. "Quint has search and arrest warrants. Charlene Rhoades Shipley will be out of business at 9 a.m."

Dotty grabbed her purse. "I'll see everyone at the courthouse."

CJ gnawed on her lip as she drove to the courthouse in Angleton, the county seat. What had they missed? The plan seemed solid, but unexpected things could always crop up. She whispered a mantra David preached to her when she came out of the highway patrol academy. "Plan, but be ready to adapt."

She pulled David's work vehicle into a parking space reserved for law enforcement. A small army of reporters gathered on the north side of the courthouse.

"Dotty drew a crowd," said CJ as she strode toward the steps. She noticed the sheriff standing at the door, looking like a buzzard ready to swoop down on a dead rabbit.

Quick steps brought her inside to a metal detector where she pulled out her badge and identification. Raised eyebrows and a nod were the only response from a low-ranking deputy. Instead of heading into the courtroom, CJ waited in the hallway.

THE MINIVAN EASED into a parking space a block away from the courthouse. David turned to Jessica before he reached for the door handle. "Are you ready?"

Jessica's head bobbed up and down. "It's time for me to put into practice what I learned in theater classes."

She looked in the mirror and pushed out her lips until they took on the appearance of a seductive pout. Her whole body assumed the character of a woman designed to draw attention in every way except with her words.

David's cell phone came to life. Jessica let out a squeal borne of nervousness. The caller ID read Amy Stewart.

"What's wrong?" asked David.

"Charlie isn't here."

"Does she sometimes come in late on Monday?"

"She's never late."

"Did Quint and the troopers get everything they came for?"

"Yes."

"Good. Thanks, Amy."

Jessica stiffened. David turned to her. "Charlene didn't show up to work this morning. Something's going on. Tell CJ to stay on her toes."

David put on sunglasses, stuffed a tie into the pocket of a sports coat and opened the van door. "Go in the south door." He pointed. "It's away from all the activity. I'll be behind you. No matter what happens, don't look at me."

The deep-cut knit top Jessica wore should have had a camisole under it. It didn't. The form fitting skirt should have been two inches longer. It wasn't. The three-inch high heels showed off shapely, tanned legs. She retrieved a bottle of extravagantly expensive perfume and applied it like cheap aftershave.

Jessica's practiced runway walk, an I-could-care-less swagger, accentuated her presence. She ascended the courthouse steps with David a few feet behind her. Caught in the cloud of fragrance he stifled a sneeze.

No one noticed him in his dress slacks, black shoes, long sleeve dress shirt, cheap sports coat, sunglasses and the ridiculous baseball cap with a pony tail dangling out the back. Jessica stopped to ask where the hearing for Mr. Quisenheimer would be held after she'd cleared the metal detector. The deputy waved David through without looking at his face. A green light and the absence of a high-pitched squeal from the machine sufficed for security.

The men's room lay straight ahead on the left. With Jessica leading the way, David concluded he could have been painted purple and no one would have noticed him.

CJ CHOKED BACK a smile when she saw how little attention people paid to David as he ducked into the restroom. She whispered to the beauty as she passed, "Great job. Save seats for Dotty and me on the back row. I'll stay in the hallway for now."

"David said for you to stay on your toes. Charlene didn't show for work this morning."

CJ mumbled to herself. "Make your plan, then adapt."

A captain and a lieutenant flanked the sheriff when they entered the courthouse ten minutes before the proceedings were to begin. The courtroom had three hall entrances to cover. Each of the men took one. CJ stood near the open main door to the courtroom and found herself within feet of the sheriff. Her throat constricted as her hands became suddenly moist.

Minutes passed before the sounds of an all-out media frenzy tumbled up the steps and into the courthouse. Quint Fowler and a highway patrol sergeant gripped each of Bob's arms. A glare from Quint to the deputy manning the metal detector insured they would not be asked to tarry as they walked through the device and sent it screaming.

The trooper sergeant, a mountain of a man, approached the sheriff. The officer with chevrons on his sleeves uncoupled his hand from his prisoner and blocked the sheriff's view of Bob. It happened so fast the sheriff didn't have time to get a good view of Robert Quisenheimer. Down the center aisle strode the Texas Ranger and the wrongly convicted man. Conversations buzzed throughout the courtroom.

With a full minute to spare, Bob took his seat beside his attorney, Clive Rosenberg. Stephen Shipley looked on, exchanged brief smiles with his friend's father, and returned his gaze to papers on his desk.

CHAPTER THIRTY-EIGHT

David slid the latch on the second-to-last stall in the men's room. He removed the hat and dark glasses and hung them on a coat hook inside the stall. The pre-knotted tie slipped over his head. With the jacket covering his shirt, he put on eyeglasses and completed the transformation into his father's twin.

He remembered an overlooked detail and reached into the breast pocket of the sports coat to retrieve his cell phone. Startled by it ringing, David juggled the phone like a hot potato, controlled it, and pushed the button that allowed communication.

"This is Brian Boxwhite. Charlene and Judge Rhoades came in this morning and cleaned out your mom and dad's safety deposit boxes."

"When?"

"They got here a little before nine and left a few minutes ago."

David paused as his mind slipped into high gear. He looked at his watch. Five after ten. "Why did it take so long?"

"They had to make multiple trips. Whatever she and her

dad were putting in those bags must have weighed a ton. Charlie dripped with sweat by the time they left."

"Did they clean out the checking and savings accounts, too?"

"Everything. They demanded cash. That's what took so long. The teller made a mistake in counting it and had to start over."

"Thanks, Brian. I owe you."

"No problem. Pay me back by coming home more often."

David sat in the bathroom stall and wove together a plan of action. He punched in a text to CJ. "*Charlene & judge cleaned out all bank accounts. Follow judge after hearing. Don't let him get away.*"

AT TEN-THIRTY JUDGE RHOADES entered the courtroom through a side door. The bailiff commanded everyone to rise as the judge's gavel slammed down and brought the room to order. The room's occupants took their seats amid a noisy shuffle.

CJ leaned to one side so she could get a better view of the man who had so harmed her husband. The judge didn't look evil. She guessed him to be of average height and weight. Balding slightly, a little more hook to the nose than most, but other than that, just another man. No horns. No pitchfork.

A fist of iron in a velvet glove soon became apparent. "Before I proceed, I want to express how disappointed I am in our judicial system in general. In particular, I condemn the shoddy work of the district attorney. Had the appeal been handled properly, the outcome would be much different. Before the good citizens trusted me to be their judge, I prosecuted the man who sits at the defendant's table. He's as guilty today as the day he murdered his wife."

CJ winced. Clive Rosenberg rose to object to the proceedings. Before he could speak, the judge cut him off. "Counselor, before you say one word, I'm going to warn both you and this sorry excuse for an assistant district attorney. If either of you interrupt me, I'll have you held in contempt of court."

Stephen Shipley stood to his feet. "Your Honor, how much will that fine be?"

The judge didn't hesitate. "Young man, that question will cost you one hundred dollars."

Stephen smiled and replied, "Well worth it, Your Honor. I'd pay the district clerk but I understand she's going to be tied up for some time to come."

CJ covered her mouth to stuff back a laugh. The reporters made less of an attempt. Blood rose in the judge's face until it met his receding gray hair.

"Bailiff, remove this man from my courtroom."

Clive Rosenberg found his voice. "Judge, you can't. According to the Texas Code of Criminal Procedure—"

The judge raised his voice. "Don't you be quoting law or procedure to me, counselor."

He regained a semblance of composure and continued. "All right, I'll play the money game with you." He made a teepee of his fingers. "Every time either of you speak, I'll double your fine. Mr. Shipley, you now owe two hundred dollars and Mr. Rosenberg, you're fined one hundred dollars."

Clive sprung to his feet again, "But, Your Honor—"

The judge interrupted with a slam of the gavel. "Now you're both at two hundred. Does anyone want to raise it to four hundred?" He paused. "I didn't think so."

People in the courtroom froze in place. "Now, where was I? Oh, yes. I examined all evidence available at the time and what's been presented since Robert Quisenheimer willfully and deliberately murdered his wife. That's what the jury ruled and I've seen nothing to contradict that verdict. Let me lay out the evidence."

The judge droned on. CJ leaned into Dotty and whispered, "He's stalling. He doesn't need to be doing this. It's not going to change the outcome. Why won't he get on with it?"

Dotty lifted her shoulders and let them fall.

"Twelve honest men and women examined the evidence. The jury reached a unanimous verdict on the first vote. I still believe he is a danger to society. Therefore, at the conclusion of this hearing, I'm ordering this man be taken into custody as the sheriff investigates other serious crimes that occurred in the county prior to the murder of June Quisenheimer."

A gasp came from the gallery and the judge looked down at something in his hand. He continued, "Despite my personal belief of this man's guilt in the murder of his wife, we are a state and nation of laws. The rule of law must be upheld. Therefore, in the matter before us today, I have signed the order issued by the Court of Criminal Appeals. Robert Quisenheimer, you are hereby found not guilty of murder and released on that charge. Bailiff, take this man into custody. This hearing is concluded." The gavel fell a final time, and the judge scurried out a side door.

CJ spun to face Jessica and Dotty. "He received a text message. That's why he stalled so long. We have to get Dad to the bathroom before the sheriff's men can get to him." Both women nodded.

Quint Fowler took Bob by the arm and plowed a path for him to the back of the courtroom. The burly sergeant blocked a bailiff from getting a hand on Bob. CJ, Jessica and Dotty pushed into the aisle ahead of Quint. The sheriff stood in the doorway with a folded piece of paper jutting from his shirt pocket. CJ gave a nod to the women. They linked arms and ran forward. The sheriff tried to sidestep and push his way past her, but CJ cut him off. She jerked her knee upward at the perfect moment and he doubled over in pain. The three determined women kept him hemmed in until Quint and Bob stepped past. Dotty jerked the folded paper from his pocket. CJ gave the women a quick head nod toward an exit. Dotty and Jessica beat a hasty retreat as a sea of reporters swarmed the sheriff, demanding answers.

CJ broke away and trailed Quint and Bob down the hallway toward the men's room. A sheriff's captain stepped in front of Quint. "We have a warrant for this man's arrest."

"You do? Let me see it."

"The sheriff has it."

"While you're looking for it, he's going to the restroom. When he's finished, we'll talk."

Quint opened the restroom door. Only Bob entered.

CJ turned her back to the approaching sheriff. Over her shoulder, she heard, "Where is he? I have an arrest warrant."

"Where is it?" asked Quint in a voice that conveyed no hint of distress. Television crews captured the chaos of the scene as it unfolded.

Quint continued when the sheriff couldn't produce the warrant. "It doesn't matter. If you say there's a warrant, then there's a warrant. Here's your man now."

Dressed identically to his father, wearing theatrical make up and glasses with clear lenses, David entered the hall with knees bent and shoulders rounded forward.

"Robert Quisenheimer, you're under arrest," crowed the sheriff. David held his hands straight out in front of him to receive handcuffs. Attorney Clive Rosenberg played his part by giving a boisterous objection. He concluded his protest by stating, "Don't worry, Bob. I'll have you out as soon as I find out how much bail is. They're not going to do this to you again."

Flanked by deputies, CJ looked on as the sheriff led David away from the men's room. The glare of cameras and the roar of shouted questions continued until the throng disappeared from sight.

Quint stood guard as CJ gave the secret knock on the door. Stripped of coat, tie and dress shirt, Robert Quisenheimer exited the restroom wearing a tie-dyed T-shirt. CJ couldn't help but giggle at the baseball cap with the absurd bushy-blond hair sticking out the sides and the pony tail trailing out the back.

"Dad, you look like a hold-over from a sixties rock concert."

"Groovy, let's blow this pad."

Quint Fowler pulled a cell phone from his ear and slipped it in his coat pocket. "Everything at the county jail is going according to plan. State troopers have taken over. As soon as the sheriff pulls into the sally port, we'll take him down and get David out."

CJ nodded her approval. "Dad and I are going to follow the judge. I'll call you if anything unusual happens." CJ turned to her father-in-law. "Come on, Dad, the judge has a head start on us. I think I know where he's going."

CHAPTER THIRTY-NINE

Once away from the court house, David began his questions from the back seat of the sheriff's car. "Is this the way to the county jail?"

"Sure is," sneered the sheriff.

David chose his words with care. "Something tells me I may have an accident this time around."

The captain sitting beside the sheriff let out a jagged laugh. "It won't be an accident. You're going to be found with a shank sticking in you about an hour from now. Don't you remember? You made a lot of enemies while you were in prison."

David allowed quiet to fill the car before he continued. "Aren't you afraid someone will get a little suspicious of all the knives?"

The sheriff looked in the rear-view mirror. "What do you mean?"

David shrugged as he continued to impersonate his father. "First June, then Samuel Barcroft, now me. Every time it's with a knife. Rangers look for patterns. They're on to you."

The sheriff stared in the rear-view mirror. "You may not believe this, but I felt bad about what I did to your wife."

"Yeah, I bet." David dangled bait in front of the sheriff.

"I really did. She wasn't supposed to be there. We checked your house every day for a week."

The captain chimed in, "Your wife always stayed gone until noon. Why did she have to come home that morning?"

The question hung in the air as David flexed his fists. He wanted to end the remembrance of his mother's death, but not before he heard a full confession.

"Let me guess, you took Samuel Barcroft out of county jail to do the burglary. June walked in on him and he couldn't leave her alive."

"That's right," said the sheriff. "By the time we got there, Barcroft had made a real mess of things. What I did counts as a mercy killing."

David hung his head. "All this because of an invention intended to be a joke. It could never work."

Before the sheriff could stop him, the captain blurted out. "Judge Rhoades sure thought it would. That daughter of his had him convinced."

"Shut up," barked the sheriff. "I've had enough of this trip down memory lane."

The sheriff took another long look in the mirror. A light of recognition came into his eyes and a panicked voice screeched, "Who are you?"

At that moment David knew he would never make it to the county jail. He needed to stall.

"Sheriff, I'm a special assistant to the Texas Rangers. I'm also Robert Quisenheimer's son." David paused as an idea came alive. Words flowed smooth and sure. "Shouldn't you be getting to the judge's house?"

The sheriff's eyebrows narrowed. "Why should I do that?"

David and the sheriff stared at each other in the mirror. "You might not want anyone else to hear this."

"Keep talking. I'll decide who needs to listen."

David leaned forward. "Judge Rhoades and Charlene Shipley cleaned out their bank accounts this morning. They also took everything in my parents' safe deposit boxes."

The sheriff jerked his head up to look into his prisoner's eyes. "You're lying. You couldn't know that."

"Would I be here if the Rangers hadn't figured out everything you and the judge and Charlene have been doing? My dad and I had a nice vacation with Quint Fowler in a bay house this weekend. In fact, state troopers are running your jail as we speak." David leaned back and tried to appear relaxed. "You might as well give up. The judge has all the money. That includes your cut. I received a phone call while the judge performed that circus act of a hearing. Brian Boxwhite—you know Brian, don't you, Sheriff? The bank president? Anyway, Brian called me and told me Charlene wore herself out carrying bags of something heavy from the bank this morning. She and the judge demanded cash for everything in their checking and savings accounts."

"You're lying."

He needed one more thing to seal the deal. David took a chance. "I bet the judge had you clean out the safe in your office and bring him the money this weekend."

The proverbial straw settled on the sheriff's back. David could almost hear it break. He didn't stop. "It's over, Sheriff. State troopers will have you cuffed and stuffed before sundown and the judge and Charlene will be drinking something tall and cool on a tropical beach."

Fingers raked through short salt and pepper hair. "This can't be true. You wouldn't be telling me about it. The Rangers would've already arrested me."

"We figured you'd do anything to kill my father. I had to

get him to safety first. That's what I did." David leaned forward. "I bet the judge is warming up his airplane right now. He'll be spending your money while you face the music."

The sheriff yanked the steering wheel and pulled off the road. "Check him for a wire. If he's transmitting what we said, our goose is cooked."

The captain's boot scuffed the ground before the car came to a complete stop. He yanked open the back door.

"He's wired. Old school. Not a transmitter, just a small recorder. Real cheap."

"Give it to me," shouted the sheriff.

The captain tossed the device in the front seat and prepared to get in when the sheriff stopped him. "Check that back door. Make sure it's closed."

As soon as the captain reached for the back-door handle, the sheriff floored the accelerator on the unmarked car.

David turned to see a bewildered captain with one hand on his weapon.

"Hey, this isn't the way to the new county jail," complained David.

"Change of plans," barked the sheriff. "I need to talk with the judge."

CHAPTER FORTY

Bob held on as CJ took a corner at a speed that caused the tires and her father-in-law to squeal. "Holy smoke," said the wide-eyed man. "Keep in mind I haven't had a chance to get health insurance yet."

"Relax, Dad. They trained me at the Highway Patrol Academy."

"How many years ago?"

"David told me not to let the judge get away, no matter what. He has a good reason for saying that."

CJ slowed as the judge's car moved onto a county road. "I know where he's going. We don't have to follow so close."

"Thank goodness. I've not been thrown around so much since they closed Astroworld."

CJ couldn't help but smile. In her mind, she painted a picture of Bob and June taking David to an amusement park.

"Where's the judge going?" asked Bob.

"To his home. It's three miles down this road. Slide your hand under the seat. David keeps binoculars there."

They passed the judge's estate and then the sheriff's driveway. With a spin of the wheel and a quick acceleration, the back end of David's SUV traded places with the front. CJ drove a short distance and pulled off the road as Bob looked through binoculars.

"Uh-oh," declared Bob. "There's a twin-engine airplane leaving the hanger. The judge parked his car at the far end of the runway and is outside waiting for the plane."

CJ jerked her cell phone from her pocket and hit the name Quint Fowler.

Quint answered on the first ring. "What's wrong?"

"Twin-engine airplane leaving hanger. It appears to be preparing for take-off," responded CJ.

"Whatever you have to do, don't let that plane take off. Our intended guests never showed up. I'm on my way and so is every state trooper I can find."

Another name came to CJ's mind. She called Dotty, explained the situation and gave her the location.

CJ breathed deep to get her emotions under control. She looked to her right at the man she now called Dad. He fine-tuned the binoculars and looked down a long runway.

"They're taxiing away from us, getting ready to turn into the wind. Catherine, we'll never make it through that steel gate. It looks like they're almost to the end of the runway. Wait, it stopped. The door is opening for the judge and his daughter. We still have a little time. They're carrying bags of something from a car."

CJ gritted her teeth, turned off the motor, and burst from the door. "They are not getting away. Not today." Quick strides took her to the rear of the vehicle. Bob opened his door and joined her. She opened the larger of two rifle cases.

Bob's eyes widened. "Where did David get that canon?"

"This is one of his sniper rifles."

"Can you shoot that thing?"

"It's a Barrett fifty caliber. I'm nowhere near as good as David. It kicks like a mule." CJ hesitated as she folded out two support legs on the front of the rifle. She steadied her aim on the car's hood. "Give me a distance, Dad."

"I've been looking at the inside of a jail cell, not distances. I guess it's about a mile?" He looked through the binoculars again. "You'd better hurry, the plane is kicking up dust."

"No time for adjustments. Here goes nothing."

"They're starting to roll."

CJ sent a round into the chamber and settled her cheek against the stock. The plane gained speed. CJ took in a deep breath, let it out, took in another and held it. She placed the cross hairs of the scope on the plane's front tire and gently squeezed.

The rifle bucked upward. CJ rocked back and tried to regain her vision in the scope.

Before she could see if her shot hit, Bob squealed with delight and danced in a circle. "Perfect shot! The entire left wheel assembly collapsed. The plane slid off the runway. They aren't going anywhere."

"Did you say I hit the left wheel?"

"Tore it to pieces."

"Great. I aimed at the front tire. Don't tell David."

Bob slapped her on the back. "It'll be our little secret."

With all her attention on the airplane, CJ didn't see the sheriff's car approach. The crash of the cruiser hitting the front gate caused her to jerk her head to the left. The iron barricade to the judge's kingdom had been breached.

"Come on. David's in that car." With the radio microphone in hand she depressed the button. "All units, be advised: A car breached front gate of Judge Rhoades' property and is headed for landing strip and airplane. Be advised the sheriff has a hostage. Repeat, there's a state trooper being held hostage."

The radio traffic wouldn't go unnoticed by the eager reporters Dotty had already notified.

"Dad, when we get to the runway, I'm going to park so the car will protect you. Get behind the front tire and sit on the ground. If there's any shooting, it'll have to go through the engine to hit you."

"Where will you be?"

"I'm trading this rifle for David's assault rifle. I'll join you at the front tire."

"Is this an SUV or a gun safe?"

"Both." CJ couldn't help but smile despite the concern for her husband. "You and David are so much alike. You both respond to tense situations with wise cracks."

"He and I should be able to write a best-selling joke book after today."

As they passed through the mangled gate Bob observed, "Not quite as well constructed as it appeared."

CJ sped up to forty-five on the asphalt ribbon that ran parallel to the runway. She whipped the SUV to the right, cut a path through grass and found traction again when the tires reached the tarmac.

"Catherine, the sheriff's out of his car. He's pointing his pistol at the airplane."

"I see him."

The door to the aircraft opened. The judge bounded down the stairs with pistol in hand.

"He has a gun, too," yelled Bob.

The sheriff and the judge stood twenty yards apart, spraying bullets at each other.

CJ keyed the microphone and declared to the world, "ACU-02 to all units. Shots fired. Step it up." She dared not drive any closer to what looked like a video game gunfight. The brakes shuddered the vehicle to a stop. She cut the wheel to the right at the last second. The car sat broadside to the dual.

The shattering of glass on the sheriff's windshield caused her heart to miss a beat. "David!"

Bob exited his door and sat with his back to the front tire. CJ sprinted to the rear of the vehicle where she retrieved a black rifle. She slammed home a thirty-round clip and yanked back the bolt. With finger ready to release the safety, she approached Bob.

A lull in the shooting gave her the opportunity she waited for and she raised her rifle.

The sheriff fumbled on his belt for a fresh clip. The judge looked down at his empty pistol as if it had betrayed him.

"Drop your weapons," commanded CJ. "I haven't shot anyone in quite a while. Today seems like a real good day for it."

Both men swiveled their heads toward the new threat. The judge responded by dropping his revolver. "Shoot that man. I'm a state judge. He tried to kill me."

"You lying, no good thief!" The sheriff tossed his pistol at the judge and ran toward him.

The two men grappled on the runway like seventh-grade boys vying for the same cute girl. Charlene exited the plane and came to her father's defense with curses, kicks and wild punches.

"Dad, go check on David." Bob had already left his hiding place.

While the trio of unlikely pugilists scraped knuckles, elbows, and knees, CJ let them fight. She watched as Bob yanked opened the back door of the sheriff's car.

"David, are you all right?"

The muffled sounds of her husband's voice came forth. "I'm all right, Dad. But I'm wedged in. Give me a hand."

CJ kept the muzzle of the rifle pointed toward the fighters.

Bob plopped down on the ground and let out a relieved

"Whew." He paused, mussed David's hair and grinned. "This reminds me of the time you got stuck behind the washing machine. Let's see, you were four. Do you remember that?"

"Can we talk about this later?"

"There's no rush. That wife of yours is quite capable of handling the three stooges."

"Dad!" David said with more force.

"Oh, all right. Give me your hand." Tugs and pulls followed until David emerged. He stood straight and scanned the scene as the screams of sirens approached.

The first of a procession of highway patrol cars arrived, followed closely by news crews. A state trooper advanced to break up the fight, but halted when David held up his hands in a gesture for him to stop.

Still handcuffed, David approached CJ. She stuck the muzzle of the rifle in the air and kissed her husband like she meant it.

"Good to see you, too, Mrs. Harper." He looked at the trio who had fought their way to the grass beside the landing strip. "I see you didn't try to break it up."

"Nope," replied CJ. "The news crews need footage."

Before long, the trio had punched themselves into exhaustion. After CJ released her husband from the sheriff's handcuffs, David approached his mother's murderer and slapped them on the sheriff's wrists. With hands cuffed behind him, David led the sheriff to the car with the shot-out windshield and pointed. "Check out your dash camera. Tell me if anything looks different."

"I'm not saying anything without a lawyer."

"No problem. I'll do all the talking." He pointed to the camera mounted to the dashboard. "I made some adjustments last night. You'll notice it points in the wrong direction. I rigged it so it came on as soon as you started the engine. Everything you did or said in the car is recorded.

Thanks for the confession. You'll be able to watch it at your trial."

The sheriff's eyes opened wide before they closed to evil slits.

"That's right, Sheriff. I have your confession that you murdered my mother. You also said the judge ordered the burglary."

David paused and geared up for a final insult. "And you call yourself a lawman? You unloaded fifteen rounds at a man directly in front of you. You didn't come close to hitting him. You're pathetic."

David motioned and a state trooper took the sheriff to a waiting cruiser.

CJ sidled up next to him and his grin broadened.

Her relief made a sharp turn when he said, "There's not another female officer on site. Charlie needs to be searched and with all the news crews here, we don't want to be accused of anything that might be misconstrued as not following protocol."

CJ asked with more than a little disgust in her voice, "Are there any other old girlfriends you'd like me to frisk while I'm at it?"

CHAPTER FORTY-ONE

T he first breath of fall blew in from the north, crossed the river, crept up the gentle slope, and eased over the back porch of the Harper's home. Bea and CJ made claim to the swing while David, Billy Paul and Bob settled on lawn chairs and nursed after-dinner cups of coffee.

"Bob, are you still living in the barn?" asked Billy Paul.

"I wouldn't have it any other way. Prison is one of the noisiest places you can imagine. Cussing and hollering and people acting a fool. Sounds bounce off every wall and concrete floor. At night the snoring of a row of men is a cacophony unlike any you've ever heard. I'm enjoying the peace and quiet. Besides, I'm getting the barn whipped into shape."

David lowered his coffee mug. "There's something about engineers. It drives them crazy if one tool or part isn't in its proper place and labeled."

"Guilty as charged," said Bob. "But now you can find whatever you're looking for."

"Speaking of guilty as charged. What's the latest on all that mess down in Brazoria County?" asked Billy Paul.

CJ fielded the question. "It's about what you'd expect. Judge Rhoades lawyered up. He won't say a word. Since he cleaned out all his bank accounts and tried to leave the country, he has no money. Most of his assets were in cash and gold. It's evidence for the upcoming trials and he can't touch it."

"Serves him right," said Billy Paul. "How long will it take to get things straightened out?"

David shrugged. "The system works slow. It'll take at least a year because of all the mixed-up money and gold. He'll have to rely on a court-appointed attorney or represent himself and there's no chance of release on bond after he tried to fly away. I seriously doubt he'll ever be a free man again."

"And the sheriff?" asked Bea.

"The sheriff didn't take kindly to the judge trying to make off with all the loot and leave him alone to face the music. He gave Quint Fowler and the special prosecutor plenty on what the judge did and how he did it."

"Tell them about your old girlfriend," said Bob.

David nodded. "And then there's Charlie, the judge's daughter. I can't help but feel sorry for her. She's out on bond. Her attorney is doing her best to strike a deal with the prosecutors."

"Why not?" asked Billy Paul.

"She's agreed to turn state's evidence and testify that her dad forced her do what she did." David took a sip of coffee. "Surprisingly, she has a pretty good case by making herself out to be a victim. Who knows, she might get a probated sentence."

Bea shook her head. "I don't get it. She started the whole thing when she told her daddy about the gold magnet."

"She's claiming her father traumatized her. It's something like the battered woman syndrome defense."

"How'd he traumatize her?"

"By controlling every aspect of her life from the cradle

until three weeks ago. I was the fair-haired suitor for his daughter until she told him about the gold magnet."

Billie Paul scratched his head. "I'm still not clear on how Charlie stole the money when people posted bond."

David sat back down. "Biff Stewart gave me the first clue. He told a joke about a preacher and a check in a coffin. The man who wrote the check told the preacher's friend, 'He can cash it any time he wants to.'"

David turned and scanned the group. "That joke got me to thinking. When Amy Stewart told me about the second ledger and the checks that only Charlie would make out, I understood how she did it. The video camera Amy hid in the ceiling provided the hard evidence."

Billy Paul threw up his hands. "You lost me. I still don't understand how she stole all that money."

David sat on the edge of his chair. "Let's take it step by step. The sheriff's minions would identify people in jail who were to appear before Judge Rhoades. Deals were offered. If they posted a large bond, and paid in cash, they could get either no sentence, a light punishment, or be placed on probation, even if they deserved to go to prison. The people would pay the cash bond to the district clerk's office. Charlie kept the cash in a safe in her office. After the court proceedings, the people were supposed to be refunded their cash bond. Instead of issuing the check to that person, Charlie would find the name of a recently deceased person and make the check out to them. She chose these carefully. Real checks were issued to dead people. Amy kept the books, and they always balanced because the amount of the check issued matched the amount of cash collected. The computer printout that Amy received had the name of the person to receive the check, not the dead person's name."

"Didn't the people who paid the cash bond ever complain?" asked Billy Paul.

David shrugged off the question. "The people got what they paid for: cases dismissed, probation, or release with a fine and credit for time served in county jail. If they complained, Charlie told daddy and the sheriff paid them a visit."

"Where did the cash go then?"

David pointed a finger at his father. "Charlie took the cash and put it in Mom and Dad's safe deposit boxes."

"Why Charlie?" asked Billy Paul.

"The judge needed to put as much distance between him and those deposit boxes as he could. When Charlie reached her majority, he made her the executor of mom and dad's estate and took himself off the signature cards at the bank. With Dad in prison, Mom dead, and me nowhere in sight there was no one to question who he made executor of the estate."

Bob added, "Don't forget son, the sheriff cleaned out his safe every so often."

"That's right. The judge made sure he received his cut from what the sheriff managed to extort with all his schemes. That cash also went into Mom and Dad's safe deposit boxes."

Billy Paul spoke next. "There's something I don't understand. In the newspaper it said that airplane carried a whole lot of gold. Why gold?"

David leaned back in his chair. "Why don't you tell them, Dad?"

Bob nodded. "When I developed my make-believe gold magnet, I did a lot of research. I learned about the metallurgical properties of gold and I also learned it's viewed as a nearly universal currency that's virtually untraceable. Dollar bills have serial numbers. They also take up more space than gold."

Billy Paul nodded, "I see where this is headed."

Bob continued, "The judge believed the magnet would

work and decided to send the sheriff to steal my plans. All they had to do was find a skilled burglar, release him from jail for a couple of hours, tell him what to do and check him back into jail. They didn't plan on June coming home."

Bob heaved a sigh. "Of course, the plans for the gold magnet were worthless. But the judge saw gold as an appreciating asset that could be easily transported and exchanged for whatever currency, goods or services he wanted. Gold fit more neatly into his deceptive plan than a safe full of currency. Whenever his cash stockpile got over a half million dollars, he'd fly to the Caribbean and purchase gold. He brought it back on his airplane and stored it in my safe deposit boxes."

David added, "And who's going to question a state judge taking his daughter on a vacation to the Caribbean?"

Billy Paul had a final question. "What happens to all the gold? Who gets it?"

David stood and grinned. "Who knows? The courts will have to decide how much of it belongs to Dad."

Billy Paul squinted. "Didn't that gold come out of Bob and June's safe deposit boxes?"

David nodded.

"And there's no way of telling what was in there before they shanghaied Bob off to prison?"

"That's right," said David.

"And there aren't too many folks asking for refunds from the contraband brought into the jail, or from the jail escapes, or from posting bond on sentences they didn't get much punishment for, are there?"

Billy Paul scratched his chin. "I'd be surprised if anyone comes forth to make a claim." He paused and looked at Bob. "Mr. Harper, you did invent a gold magnet."

CJ's determined to bring her officer's killer to justice...
No matter the cost.
Can she stop him, or will she be next?

A MURDER REDEEMED
EXCERPT

Thick, sticky night air closed in as soon as CJ opened the door to the University Police Department. Distant flashes of lightning gave warning of an approaching wet, cold front. Once again, the weatherman had underestimated the speed of the front. She hoped to be home before it hit. Needing rest to function at the regents' meeting the following day, she longed for relief from her cough and a full night's sleep.

David led the way to his SUV. She alternated her gaze between David's stride and the truck. Everything ached.

"Thanks for bringing me supper. Too bad I couldn't eat any of it. Anyway, the throat lozenges are helping," said CJ.

"If you don't get to bed, you'll be joining John in the hospital."

A chill shot through her. "I feel awful. It sprinkled last night when I was hiding in the bushes watching the parking lot between Mesquite Hall and the library."

"Go home now. And it's straight to bed with you."

She shook her head and grimaced. It pounded as if miners were wailing away with pickaxes, but she needed to finish preparing for tomorrow's meeting.

"You're one hard-headed woman," said David with a huff. "Stop worrying." He took a step closer and reached for her arm.

She held up a hand with an open palm. "Don't get too

close. I don't want you getting whatever I have. After tomorrow's meeting, I'll be able to rest."

The first rumble of distant thunder rolled across the fields and through campus. Livestock from the Ag Department across the street made for the sanctuary of the lee side of barns. Another shiver shook CJ from head to waist.

Tires squealed as an older burgundy Camaro took a corner too fast and headed toward their location. A trailing patrol car activated pulsating red and blue lights. Both vehicles came to rest forty yards past the police department.

"Who's making the stop?" asked David.

"Sloan. It's his last day before he goes to work at Riverview P.D."

"At least you're getting rid of one problem."

She gave her head a slow nod as she kept her eyes on Sloan. He approached the driver. "You know, I tried to work with him, but..."

What sounded like a string of exploding firecrackers shattered the calm of the evening. Sloan slumped to the ground. The Camaro's tires smoked and screeched as they fought to gain traction. Sloan raised his pistol and fired a single round.

CJ had her .40 caliber Glock in her hand and was raising it when David yelled, "Hold fire!" She glanced to her right to see him staring down the sights of his .357 caliber Model 19.

"Houses down range. Can't risk it," said David.

Obscured by trees lining the street, the sports car squealed around a corner and sped off campus.

CJ keyed her microphone. "ACU-02 to all units. Shots fired. Officer down. Repeat. ACU-02 to all units. Shots fired. Officer hit. Officer down. Roll EMS to ACUPD. Suspect vehicle is a burgundy Camaro. Approach with extreme caution. Suspect armed with fully automatic weapon."

By the time she finished her broadcast, she had sprinted

halfway to where the officer lay. David's SUV flew past her with lights pulsing and siren screaming.

Sloan lay on his back, pistol held loose in his hand. Blood flowed from his right thigh and lower abdomen, and gushed from his neck.

"Tell EMS to step it up," shouted CJ into her microphone.

Her hands cupped over the worst of the wounds. She applied as much pressure as she could to the tear in his neck. Blood oozed from between her fingers as it pulsed against her palm. She dared not pull back her hands. Questioning eyes looked up at her.

Too much blood. It saturated and spread from his uniform into pools on the street. Its sticky dampness soaked her knees as she knelt beside him.

The *Star of Justice Series* is available in paperback and ebook at your favorite online retailer.

About the Author

Drawing from his extensive background in criminal justice, Bruce Hammack writes contemporary, clean read detective and crime mysteries. He is the author of the Smiley and McBlythe Mystery series and the Star of Justice series. Having lived in eighteen cities around the world, he now lives in the Texas hill country with his wife of thirty-plus years.

Follow Bruce on Bookbub and Goodreads for the latest new release info and recommendations. Learn more at brucehammack.com.

Just for mystery lovers!
Receive a free mystery short story when you sign up for Bruce's newsletter at brucehammack.com.

Thank you for reading one of my books. I hope the mystery and suspense kept you turning the page to see what happens next. If you enjoyed the book, please take a minute to leave a review at your favorite retail site, Bookbub or Goodreads. Reviews help other readers discover a great read and help your favorite authors keep churning out stories for you to enjoy.

Happy Reading!

Bruce